William Collings Lukis De Guérin

Huguenot Guérins and Their Descendants

Together with biographical sketches of others of the name

William Collings Lukis De Guérin

Huguenot Guérins and Their Descendants
Together with biographical sketches of others of the name

ISBN/EAN: 9783337289218

Printed in Europe, USA, Canada, Australia, Japan

Cover: Foto ©Raphael Reischuk / pixelio.de

More available books at **www.hansebooks.com**

AND

THEIR DESCENDANTS:

TOGETHER WITH

BIOGRAPHICAL SKETCHES

OF

OTHERS OF THE NAME.

BY

WILLIAM COLLINGS LUKIS GUÉRIN.

For Private Circulation only.

LONDON:
WATERLOW & SONS, PRINTERS, GREAT WINCHESTER STREET.
1874.

Fac-simile of an Old Wood Engraving, representing Guérin, Count of Montglave, and another Noble guarding the tent of the Emperor Charlemagne. Taken by the kind permission of the authorities of the British Museum.

𝕯𝖊𝖉𝖎𝖈𝖆𝖙𝖊𝖉

TO

ELIAS THOMAS GUÉRIN, Esquire,

Le Mont Durant, Guernsey.

TO

ELIAS THOMAS GUÉRIN, Esquire,

Le Mont Durant, Guernsey.

My dear Uncle,

In dedicating these Sketches to you, I desire
to testify my recognition of the valuable assistance you
have afforded in giving me the benefit of your own
researches respecting our common ancestor, the
Huguenot Daniel Guérin, and his descendants; the
possession of which was the inducement for gathering
further particulars, which led to the compiling of these
records of the family of Guérin, which I trust may be
of interest to all connected with the name.

Your affectionate Nephew,

W. C. LUKIS GUÉRIN.

London, *June*, 1873.

HUGUENOT GUÉRINS.

THE first Huguenot of the name of Guérin, of whom there is any authentic record, is one Jacob, who came over to England from Normandy in the year 1563 ; he was, in all probability, driven from his home during the terrible persecutions that followed the massacre on the 1st March in that year by order of the Duke de Guise, when 1,400 men, women, and children were foully murdered whilst holding a meeting in a barn at Vassy. Paux, in his history of that period, says that, "Although the massacre of St. Bartholomew is usually cited as the culminating horror of the time, the real St. Bartholomew was not that of 1572, but of 1562, and following years, which contain by far the most dolorous chapter in the history of the French Protestants."

We learn that Jacob Guérin, with his wife and children, was one of the eighteen families, who, headed by their pastor Hector Hamon, landed at Rye, in Sussex, where after a short stay they proceeded to Winchelsea, being desirous of remaining on the coast, in the hopes that should things take a favourable turn in France they would be enabled to return. In this small town they

could hardly obtain accommodation, much less employment, which they tried hard to procure, being willing and anxious to turn their talents to any account; not succeeding in their endeavours, they were at last compelled to come further inland, and crossed over to Canterbury. This city they determined to make their head-quarters, as here work could be found for them, through the care and kindness of the authorities.

In the memorial the Huguenots sent in to the magistrates and aldermen, asking permission to reside within the walls of the city, they set forth that "they had relinquished their country and their worldly goods for the love of their religion, and earnestly desired to be allowed a place to worship in, and a place set apart for the burial of their dead." This was granted, and the Crypt of the Cathedral assigned to them for their exclusive use, and to this day continues to exist as the little French Calvinist Church, wherein may be heard every Sunday the service in French, with the original Huguenot hymns, as sung upwards of three hundred years ago by the little band of exiles. It is a very simple place of worship, in accordance with the Calvinistic doctrine, fitted up with only a few pews, a pulpit, and precentor's desk; and although a dissenting chapel, it yet forms part of the high Cathedral of Canterbury. The congregation at the present time are supposed to number about twenty; the endowment of £200 a-year has, without doubt, tended to keep them together, and the little chapel in a fair state of preservation. From its early associations it must always have a peculiar interest for all in any way connected with the name of Guérin; and to any one who would desire further particulars, I would recommend a perusal of an excellent article on "The French Church in Canterbury Cathedral,"

by Samuel Smiles, to be found in "Good Words" of April, 1866.

Of the future fortunes of Jacob Guérin, or his family, we have little record, and no reliable information as to his descendants, concerning whom there are two or three surmises put forward, amongst them, that after a few years the name became Anglicised into "Gearing" or "Garing," of whom there are many in Sussex, and other parts of England. This I think very probable, as prior to 1500 in France the name was frequently written "Garin" or "Guarin." Others suppose, that in the course of a few generations they became extinct, leaving no trace behind them. But Mr. Samuel Smiles asserts as a *fact*, that "the Crofts of Sussex represent the refugee family of Guérin;" but this is a mere assumption, for which there is no foundation, except the mistake he has fallen into in supposing, that because the Crofts, a Sussex family, bore the name of "Guérin" for many generations as one of their Christian names, they must be the representatives of Jacob Guérin, who landed and lived in that county. The Crofts came by the name through a totally different source. At the revocation of the Edict of Nantes, a Peter Guérin la Plas fled to England, and some generations later a descendant of his married into the Crofts family, and "Peter" and "Guérin" were used as the Christian names of the great-grandfather, grandfather, and father of the present representative of the family, Henry Peter Crofts, Esquire, of Sompting Abbotts, near Worthing, Sussex; who most kindly showed me his family pedigree, and explained how they came by the name, and acknowledged that he had never so much as heard of Jacob Guérin, whose representative he is said to be.

I may as well introduce here émigrés of the name, who sought refuge in England from the persecutions in France about the time of the revocation of the Edict of Nantes. They appear in the lists of the Huguenots who were naturalized by letters patent, to be found in the Camden Papers.

1682. Simion Guérin, naturalized March 8th.

1682. Daniel Garin or Guérin, naturalized March 21st.

1688. Francis Guérin and Magdalene his wife, and their two children, Francis and Anne—and a Nicholas Guérin, January 5th.

1679. Solomon de Guérin and Anne his wife.

Some of these are said to have settled in Ireland, but of them or their descendants no reliable information is to be obtained.

GUÉRIN OF GUERNSEY.

This family, in its numerous branches, are the descendants of Daniel Guérin, a native of Clairac, in Agenois in Guienne, who escaped to that island during the persecutions at the time of the revocation of the Edict of Nantes.

The Guérins of Agenois, including the families at Clairac, Mairac, and Agen, hold the tradition that they came originally from another part of France—the name not being Guiennois nor Gascon, and the arms the Clairac Guérins bear, " three black lions on a gold shield," being the same as those of the Guérins of Mortagne, in Normandy. It is most probable they are a branch of the latter, who may have migrated south, and settled in Guienne, about the time this rich and fertile province was reunited to the crown of France by Charles VII., in the year 1453. The dates on the ancient title deeds still

in the possession of the Guérins of Mairac in the year 1843, coincide with this conquest, and prove that the properties had then been held by them for nearly four centuries in direct male line.

Clairac stands on the bank of the river Lot, at its junction with the Garonne; it is situated about half-way between Bordeaux and Montauban, and is in the centre of the wine-growing district. as well as the very midst of all the persecutions of 1685, and preceding years, when the whole country, from Grenoble to Bordeaux, was swept of Huguenots.

The Guérins of Clairac from the very first embraced the Protestant cause, and threw in their lot with Henry of Navarre (whose subjects, in fact, they were,) when he raised his standard as champion of the Huguenots. Their chateau was but a few leagues distance from, and plainly in view of Nerac, the favourite residence of the royal family of Navarre; and from first to last the Guérins were in the thick of the troubles of those troublous times.

Clairac itself withstood three sieges, but in each compelled the assailants, by dint of vigorous sorties, to withdraw. In one of them the Dauphin of France led the attacking party, who attempted to cross the dam in the river Lot (constructed to supply two large mills, situated at the base of the walls), but he was driven back in the desperate onslaught made by the townspeople, and when in the centre of the dam his sword was broken by a shot, his horse killed under him, and he and his followers were compelled to beat a retreat.

This broken sword, with the inscription in letters of gold, " À Monsieur Dauphin," and the breastplate of his charger, were picked up about the year 1810, when the

water of the Lot being very low, advantage was taken thereof to repair the dam, and these, as well as other arms found at the time, are deposited in the museum of the town.

Daniel Guérin was the only child of Jean Guérin, by his first wife ; by the second there were several children. Jean's father had enjoyed comparative peace, and the blessings of protection during the reign of Henry IV., and indeed for many years after the foul assassination of that king, in the year 1610 ; but Jean himself had been a witness of the defence of the town of Montauban (a few leagues distance from Clairac), where was concentrated the strength of the whole district—nobles, gentry, and people ; King Louis XIII. in person laid siege to it, but it was so successfully defended that at the end of two months he had to abandon the fruitless attempt, which frustrated all his hopes ; it is said to have caused him such grief that he left the place with tears in his eyes.

The fall of La Rochelle, the stronghold of the Huguenots, in 1628, was the death-blow to their cause as a political body ; this was followed by the Edict of Pardon, 1629, and until the accession of Louis XIV., in the year 1643, things went smoothly with the Protestants, and even then, so long as Richelieu and Mazzarin guided affairs, they did not suffer much ; it was not until after the death of these eminent men, and that of the queen-mother, in 1666, that the real persecutions commenced, culminating in 1685.

In 1683 Jean Guérin died, having lived to see the beginning of the persecutions which swept the land of the Huguenots ; and on his death-bed he earnestly besought Daniel, then about twenty years of age, and his young wife and children to remain true to the faith of their

fathers. Almost immediately after his decease the persecutions of the Protestants grew worse and worse, and by the end of two years, in the whole district around Clairac, the people, almost all Huguenots, were driven to a state of despair. From Grenoble to Bordeaux their churches were burnt down, and the congregations dispersed at the edge of the sword; week by week, month by month, the aspect of things only became blacker and blacker, and no streak of light or hope seemed to break through the heavy clouds which overhung them, till, in the summer of 1685, the climax was almost reached. A large body of troops that had been encamped on the frontier to watch the movements of the Spanish army, were now employed to assist in the "conversion," or hunting to death, of the heretics. The brutal Marquis de Louvois, having agreed upon a truce with the Spanish commander, determined to remove his soldiers into inexpensive quarters by distributing them amongst the Huguenot families. These troops were composed of the very dregs of society, and the atrocities committed by them were unparalleled; thousands of the poor victims, who were left completely at their mercy, were driven by them into the forests and wilds and caverns of the Pyrenées, there miserably to die of cold or starvation, or to be again hunted from their hiding-places. Every road and bridge were guarded by both soldiers and gendarmes, and the Catholic peasants, instigated by their priests', promises of a reward from heaven hereafter, and by the more tangible and certain reward offered by the Government for the capture of the fugitives, displayed the greatest energy in hunting up the poor Huguenots; who, when taken, were brought back heavily chained, and dragged from town to town, to strike terror into the hearts of other intending fugitives,

and afterwards sent to the galleys, irrespective of age or rank, some mere children under twelve years of age ; and there, with heavy chains round their necks, nobles, magistrates, pastors, officers, and gentlemen, were linked to the worst description of malefactors, murderers, thieves, &c., and hundreds of other poor victims were either burned to death, strangled, or thrown into the rivers with their hands and feet tied. These and other atrocities, which were in no way kept secret, but the accounts of them even exaggerated the more to impress others, were taking place on every side of Daniel Guérin, his stepmother, and her children, whilst they themselves were threatened from day to day with a fate similar to their neighbours', by having a troop of dragoons quartered on their chateau and premises, by which they would have been subjected to the grossest insults from officers as well as men, who seemed alike devoid of pity or decency ; still they refused to be converted ; anguish and terror by turns agitating their minds, they determined to remain and await the issue of events; hope almost failing them whilst contemplating the dangers by which they were surrounded, and they could not but feel that sooner or later they must decide on " conversion " or flight. The latter to Mrs. Guérin seemed worse than the former, on account of her young children ; the fatigue, privations, and extreme danger attending a flight from such a distance to the frontiers or sea-board rendered such a project almost impossible, to say nothing of the thoughts of leaving for ever the homes of their youth, and the country they so much loved ; therefore, they hesitated long, and prepared to endure much before taking the irrecoverable step. But, at last, the constant threat of having her children forcibly taken from her—the sons

to be sent to monasteries ; the daughters, like those of so many of the nobility and gentry around them, to the Convent of St. Cyr, founded especially for that purpose by Madame de Maintenon—this prospect, no doubt, drove Mrs. Guérin to desperation, and determined at least to share their fate, she yielded to the demands of her tormentors, and despite the earnest entreaties of Daniel to remain constant to the faith of her fathers, she, with her children, went to the priests, and were "converted;" abjuring their religion, but saving their lives and property, and themselves from further molestation, for on the certificate of the priests the troops were at once withdrawn from the premises of all "converts," to take up their quarters elsewhere. Hers was not a solitary instance of weakness, hundreds of other families around them were doing the same thing, yielding to the terror of the times, and the intrigues of the priests. The state of the district may be imagined from the report of the Marquis de Louvois, as to the result of his operations in this locality. It is dated September, 1685, and he writes, "Sixty thousand 'conversions' have been made in the district of Bordeaux, and twenty thousand in that of Montauban. So rapid is the progress that before the end of the month 10,000 Huguenots will not be left in the district of Bordeaux, where there were 150,000 on the 15th of last month." Clairac, as before mentioned, was just half way between Bordeaux and Montauban, and in the very heart of the persecutions which led to these rapid "conversions."

The revocation of the Edict of Nantes, published 22nd October, 1685, was the death-knell of the Huguenots, the culmination of the horrors of the persecutions in this district, and it was at this period that Daniel

Guérin made his escape. After his stepmother's "conversion," his existence became more wretched than ever; and at last under threats of serious consequences to her own children, Mrs. Guérin was persuaded by the priests to obtain an order for his arrest as a heretic. Early one morning as Jean, the faithful and aged servant of Daniel's father, was slowly descending the avenue leading to the chateau of his young master, and mournfully pondering over the dissensions which had crept into his late master's once united family, he was suddenly surrounded by a party of dragoons, who demanded whether the residence they were approaching belonged to Monsieur Daniel Guérin, and if he was at home? Suspecting the object of their mission, and aware that his young master's life probably depended on his reply, Jean answered that the estate did belong to M. Guérin, but that he was from home, and directed them to proceed to the neighbouring town of Nerac, stating that Daniel, whom he minutely described, would be found at such an hotel, whither he had gone on business. Misled by the old man's ruse, the dragoons wheeled round, and went off at a brisk pace. Jean then hastened in search of his master, to inform him of the imminent peril which he had just escaped, and conducted him with great caution to a place of concealment in some extensive caves, hidden in a secluded part of the estate and known to few or none but himself. Here, promising to bring him food and a needful disguise, the servant left him.

In the course of a few hours the dragoons, disappointed of their prey at Nerac, returned in great fury, and carefully ransacked the chateau and grounds, galloping over the extensive vineyards, hacking and destroying everything that came in their way; but after a protracted

search were finally compelled to depart without effecting
the capture they had anticipated.

When the stillness and darkness of night had set in,
some hours after the departure of the dragoons, old
Jean, who had himself been in concealment, stealthily
ventured to issue forth, and after collecting clothes,
money, and food, he hastened with all speed, by unfrequented paths, to the spot where his young master lay,
and persuaded Daniel to assume the dress of a shepherd,
which he had provided as a disguise, and to put aside
every object and article of clothing which might tend to
his identification, changing even his boots for sabots,
which had to be stuffed with moss to keep them on his
feet; then, having partaken of a hearty meal, they fell
on their knees, and, in earnest prayer, Daniel committed
himself to the protection and guidance of his Heavenly
Father.

As soon as all their preparations were finished, and
the clothes Guérin had worn hidden away in the
cave, with a most affectionate embrace and sorrowful
farewell, the old man, at the last moment, pressed on him
a purse containing his savings, which false pride did not
prevent the master from accepting, as with the trifling
amount in his own possession it was altogether but a small
sum wherewith to undertake the contemplated journey to
the frontiers, and then, by sea or land, to make an escape.

Daniel lay concealed all the following day, at night he
again started on his weary journey; and this plan he
followed for some time, resting and procuring roots, &c. for
food by day, and travelling by night, till he at last safely
crossed one of the most unfrequented defiles of the
Pyrenées, a most perilous undertaking at any time, but
especially at that period, as the whole frontier of Spain

was carefully guarded, to arrest the flight of the Huguenots, not only by the soldiers, but as before mentioned, by the peasants also, in the hopes of obtaining the large reward offered for the capture of the heretics ; numbers of whom were taken, and many escaped that fate only to meet, if possible, a worse, perishing of cold or starvation in the depths of the forests, or the fastnesses of the mountains.

Having crossed the Pyrenées, without any special incident, beyond weariness, cold, and hunger, and reached the Spanish valleys, Guérin's position was much improved, on account of his knowledge of the Spanish patois, as spoken in the Basque provinces, by which he was enabled to work his way across the country, assisting at farms, or doing anything that would procure him food and a night's lodging, without creating suspicion. Thus after many weeks of hard toil and frugal fare he at last arrived at the Portuguese frontier, which he crossed, his great object being to reach the sea-coast, and if possible to escape to England on board some ship. Through Portugal he worked his way in a similar manner, until he reached the port of Lisbon, but ere his arrival there, his last sous had long been spent, and many hours had elapsed since he had tasted food ; wayworn, faint and weary, tattered and shoeless, he hurried towards the nearest quay, where he was informed that foreign vessels were most likely to be found. To his inexpressible joy the British Ensign was floating from the mast-head of one of the first ships that met his view, but great was his surprise on approaching nearer, to hear the crew, who were busily engaged in completing the shipment of the cargo, speaking to each other in *French*. An English ship manned by a French crew, at that epoch of bitter hostility between the two nations, appeared to him a strange anomaly. After some

hesitation he ventured to enquire, and was told that the vessel hailed from Guernsey, the crew being natives of that island, but what afforded him the greatest pleasure and relief to his anxiety was, the further announcement that they, as well as their fellow-countrymen were all Protestants.

This information had scarcely been given by one of the sailors, when Mr. Peter Martin, (a partner in the house of Messrs. Carey, wine merchants, of Guernsey,) approached, and seeing a suspicious looking person in conversation with his men, demanded the nature of Guérin's business. From the reply of the seaman to this question, Daniel at once apprehended that the gentleman before him was the owner of the cargo, if not of the ship also; and stepping up to him, without any hesitation made known who and what he was, the extent of his misfortunes, and present pressing distress, begging earnestly to be allowed a passage, for which he promised to compensate the owners, as soon as he had the means of doing so.

Mr. Martin, perceiving by the expressions and manners of the unfortunate famished creature who addressed him that the coarse tattered rags concealed a gentleman of education, immediately granted his request, invited him to stay at his house until the vessel sailed, and most kindly provided him with clothes and money.

Daniel remained for some days with Mr. Martin, who took the greatest interest in him, both on account of his situation and adventures and also in consequence of his intimate knowledge of the various qualities, manufacture, and management of Claret wines, the produce of his late estate at Clairac. He then bade farewell to his host, and sailed for Guernsey, carrying with him the good wishes of his kind friend and a letter of introduction and

recommendation to Messrs. Carey, of the Brasserie, into whose service he entered in the capacity of clerk soon after his arrival in the island, in the early spring of 1686.

About this same time great numbers of the persecuted Huguenots effected their escape from the neighbouring coast of Normandy in small open fishing boats and other frail craft to avoid suspicion, and landed both in the islands of Jersey and Guernsey, after experiencing great hardships and dangers. Amongst these was Madlle. Marie Bacon, a young lady of noble descent, born at Falaise, in Normandy. The similarity of their position and misfortunes soon formed a bond of attachment and sympathy between herself and Daniel Guérin, which resulted in their union. The proceeds of the sale of a casket of jewels, which Marie Bacon had contrived to save when effecting her escape, were invested by Daniel Guérin in small commercial speculations, which so greatly prospered and increased, that in a few years, although a young family was springing up around them, Daniel was enabled to leave the employ of his kind friends the Messrs. Carey. In 1694 he purchased a house, to which in 1709 he added some land ; and at their death they left their children comfortably provided for.

Seven sons and two daughters were the issue of the marriage of Daniel Guérin and Marie Bacon, which took place at the parish church of St. Peter's Port, Guernsey, on the 22nd of December, 1686.

WILLIAM, the eldest son, was born 3rd January, 1688, and had for godfathers, William and Anthony Brock. He married, 1710, Susan Le Feuvre of the island of Serk, by whom he had one daughter, Susannah, born 1712; who married, 1729, Peter Le Massurier of Sark, by whom there was issue.

Of this Susannah Guérin there is a rather interesting anecdote told. Her mother Susan Le Feuvre had been engaged to be married to an English officer, but after their betrothment he had the misfortune to lose his hand in action, in consequence of which she refused to carry out her engagement. The disappointed officer on learning afterwards of her approaching marriage with William Guérin, expressed a hope that her first child might, like himself, have only one hand. Mrs. Guérin was unable to banish from her mind the thoughts of her own fickleness, and of her discarded lover's terrible wish, and it actually came to pass, that her only child, for she died soon afterwards, was born with but one hand.

William Guérin married, secondly, 1717, Margaret Dumaresq, by whom he had one daughter, who died unmarried.

The island of Sark at that time belonged to the Dumaresqs, a very old Jersey family. It had originally been granted by patent to Helier de Carteret, of Jersey, by Queen Elizabeth, 1564, and was held by his descendants for many generations. The silver chalice now in use in the church bears on it the inscription "Presented by Demlle. Dumaresq la Dame de Sark." The Seigneury of the island, after having passed through many hands,—those of the family of Milner, bishop of Gloucester, then to the Le Gros, through whom, by

marriage, to the Le Pelly family,—was finally purchased from the heirs of the late Ernest Le Pelly, Esquire, in the year, 1852, by Mrs. Thomas Guérin Collings; and her son the Revd. William T. Collings, M.A., is the present Seigneur.

DANIEL, born 16th January, 1690, and DOROTHY, born 26th December, 1691, died in infancy.

MATTHEW (the fourth child of Daniel Guérin and Marie Bacon), born 24th February, 1693; had for godfather Matthew Nicholas de Saumarez, and for godmother Dame Bertrame de Saumarez; (Matthew de Saumarez was the grandfather of the celebrated Admiral Lord de Saumarez). He married Mary Dagg; issue, 1, *Matthew*, 2, *John*, 3, *Mary*, and a third son, name unknown.

1. *Matthew* married Sarah Parker, by whom he had one son, *Matthew*, and two daughters;

   Sarah married Daniel Piton; and had issue.—

   Elizabeth, married Charles Marquand; and had issue.—

   Matthew, the son, first married Margaret Ollivier, of the Mont Durant; had issue one daughter, *Margaret*. By his second marriage, with Susannah de Lisle, he had one son, *Matthew de Lisle*, who died without issue.

   Margaret, married Frederick Price, by whom she had issue, 1, *Frederick*, 2, *Matthew Guérin*, 3, *Thomas*, 4, *Martha*, and 5, *Susannah Falaise*.

   Frederick, the eldest son, married Maria Vardon;

issue, *Bonamy, Vardon*, d., *Maria*, d., *Martha, Kennett, Henry, Louisa, Ann, Henrietta,* and *Frederick*, d.

Bonamy, M.A., Professor of Political Economy, Oxford, married Lydia, daughter of the Rev. Joseph Rose (her mother was the daughter of Thomas Babington, M.P., and cousin of Lord Macaulay and Lady Trevelyan); issue, *Lydia Rose*, m. James Traile Christie; *Margaret Arnold*, m. Daniel Robert Fearon; *Edith Merivale*, m. John Pickards Morley; *Mary Gertrude Stanley*; *Bertha Penrose*, m. Daniel Connor Lothbury.

Of the other children of Frederick Price, jun., I have no particulars.

2. *Matthew Guérin*, Frederick Price's second son, married a lady, name unknown; issue two sons, *Matthew* and *Edward*, and two daughters, *Mary* and *Louisa*.

3. *Thomas*, died without issue.

4. *Martha*, m. John Betts, by whom she had issue,

1. *Louisa*.

2 and 4. *William* and *James*, who died without issue.

3. *Charles*, Bey, in the Egyptian Government service, m. Eveline Pedémonti, dau. of the Italian

Consul-General in Egypt, by whom she had
issue, *Charles*, *Balfour*, *Lillie*, (m. Constanti
Sinadino), *Ida*, *Edgar*, *Amelie*, *Edwin*, *Walter*,
Arthur, and *William*.

---

5. *George Haynes*, also Bey, in the same service,
m., 1st, Margaret Finnie, who died leaving
one daughter, Amy; and secondly, Mary Ann
Collings Guérin, widow of the Rev. George
Birch.

---

6. *Caroline*, m. John Le Mottée, Jurat of the
Royal Court of Guernsey; issue,
   1. *Ada.*
   2. *Ellen*, m. F. Colville Lyon, late 43rd Regiment; issue, *Edward Colville.*
   3. *John Edward*, Captain late 64th Regiment, m., 1st, Geraldine O'Grady; and
2ndly, Laura Amelia, eldest daughter of
Frederick Collings Lukis, M.D., by
Amelia Collings his wife.
   4, *Harry*, 5, *Herbert* and 6, *Georgiana.*

---

7. *Catherine.*

---

5. *Susannah Falaise*, youngest daughter of F. Price;
died unmarried.

John Guérin (second son of Matthew by Mary Dagg),

m. 1st Mary Asty, issue, 1, *Joshua*, and 2, *Eliza-beth*; by his 2nd marriage with Elizabeth Day, he had one daughter *Mary*, who died unmarried.

1. *Joshua*, m. 1st Catherine Machon, issue, one son *Joshua* (who went to Newfoundland, and was never heard of after 1813); by his 2nd marriage with Martha Manger he had two daughters, . *Charlotte*, m. Henry Le Lacheur, and *Elizabeth*.

2. *Elizabeth*, m. Paul Bienvenu; and had issue.—

— Guérin (the third son of Matthew and Mary Dagg), married, and had one daughter, *Elizabeth*, m. William Baker, of Leamington, and had issue two sons and one daughter.

DANIEL (the 5th child of Daniel Guérin and Marie Bacon,) was born 26th April, 1694. He married Esther, daughter of John Lucas (a Huguenot refugee, residing in Jersey); issue,

Daniel, m. Thomasine Allez, of St. Martin; issue,

1, *Margaret*, married Nicholas Corbin, of La Porte; without issue.

2. *Charlotte*, m. Pierre Arnoult Des Hayes, Captain in the French Navy. He was lost on board the war sloop " Découverte." Issue dead.

3. *Elizabeth*, died unmarried.

4. *Daniel*, Commander, R.N., perished with all his crew on board the " Sirène," or " Syren," 16-gun brig, in the Bay of Honduras, in the year 1796; day unknown.

5. *George* and 6, *James*, died unmarried.

7. *Samuel*, m. Lucy Lovie : issue.
  1. *Daniel*, accidentally killed.
  2. *Samuel Allez*, m. Esther Brown : issue.
      1. *Matilda Margaret*, m. William Goodman.
      2. *Selina*, who died young, and
      3. *Frederick William*, m. Mary Blondd; issue,
          Frederick William (the present representative of the Huguenot Daniel Guérin), and *Ada*.

  3. *Guérin* Guérin m. 1st, Mary Robin; issue, *Alfred* and *Guérin*; and 2ndly, Esther Jane Bishop; issue, *Charles*, who died young.
      Alfred, m. Eliza Le Patourel; issue, 1, *Alice Rose*, m. Richard Edwyn Ozanne ; 2, *Eliza Le Patourel*; 3, *Alfred Bishop*; 4, *Nora Mauger*, and 5, *Arthur Robin*.

      Guérin, m. Ellen Stephens; issue, *Henry Robin*.

  4. *Frederick William*, died young.

Esther (daughter of Daniel Guérin and Esther Lucas), m. James Le Roy ; issue,
  James, m. Martha Lenfesty; issue, *James*, *John*, *Martha*, and *Margaret*, who all died unmarried.

Jous (6th child of Daniel Guérin and Marie Bacon), m. Margaret Ollivier, of Le Mont Durant; issue, *John* and *Isaac*, who died unmarried.

These Olliviers were a very ancient Norman family, for many centuries settled in the island of Guernsey. Their names appearing on the list of landowners made during the survey in the reign of Edward III., in the year 1331.

ELIAS (the 7th child of Daniel Guerin and Marie Bacon), born 8th Aug., 1699, m. Mary Ollivier (sister of his brother John's wife) ; issue, *Elias, Thomas,* and *Mary,* the two latter d. unmarried.

Elias, m. Mary Arnold: issue, 1, *Elias,* d.; 2, *Thomas ;* 3, *Mary ;* 4, *Margaret,* d. ; and 5, *Esther.*

Thomas, m. Susannah Price ; issue, .

    Elias, m. Mary Ann Collings, daughter of John Collings, by Margaret Mauger (see note on Collings family) ; issue,

        1, *Elias Thomas ;* 2, *Collings Mauger,* d. ; 3, *Thomas,* d. leaving issue ; 4, *William Adolphus,* d. ; 5, *Marian Sarah,* d. ; 6, *Charles Mauger,* d. ; 7, *Amelia Margaretta,* d. leaving issue ; 8, *Martha Price,* d. ; 9, *John Collings ;* 10, *Mary Ann Collings ;* 11, *Eliza Read,* d. ; 12, *Collings William,* d. ; and, 13, *Maria Matilda.*

1. *Elias Thomas* (Lieut.-Col. R. G. M.) of Le Mont Durant, m. Margueritta Sarah Collings, dau. of Rear-Admiral Sir Thomas Mansell, Kt., K.G.H., K.S.S., by Catherine Rabey Lukis, his wife, and has issue,

    1, *Elias ;* 2, *Catherine Mansell ;* and 3, *Thomas William Mansell.*

4. *Thomas*, m. Betsy Read, of the Manor of Upton Helions, Devon, for issue *see* GUÉRINS OF DEVONSHIRE.

---

7. *Amelia Margaretta*, m. the Rev. William Le Motteé, M.A., Rector of Helions Bumpstead, Essex ; issue,
    1. *William*, Capt. 18th Royal Irish, m. Ella Bell ; issue, *Florence*, *Amelia*.
    2. *Osmond*, Capt. R.A., m. Emily, dau. of Colonel Alves.
    3. *Amelia Charlotte*, d. 1867 ; 4, *Clara* ; 5, *Arthur James* ; 6, *Jessie* ; 7, *Donald* ; and 8, *Fanny*.

---

9. *John Collings* (Lieut.-Col. R. G. M.), m. Charlotte Ann, d. of the Rev. Charles Clifton (of the Northamptonshire Cliftons), of Tymaur, near Brecon, Rector of Llaufygan and Llaufraench, in the county of Breconshire.

Lieut.-Col. John Collings Guérin, whilst serving as Captain of the 1st, or East Regiment of Militia, in the year 1845, for some unknown cause, fell under the displeasure of Major-General Napier (the most eccentric Governor that ever ruled in the Channel Islands), who, on the plea that " it was not expedient for the public service that Captain Guérin should hold a commission," reduced him to the ranks as a private. The reasons for this arbitrary proceeding were refused, and Sir James Graham was appealed to in vain. Sir James, however, issued an order that no officer in the Militia of any of the Channel Islands should be dismissed in future " without the express sanction of the Secretary of State," thus significantly condemning the dismissal. Finding that Captain Guérin could obtain no redress, and that the whole matter was one of private pique, which could not bear investigation, the

officers of the Militia became most indignant, and two Lieutenant-Colonels and five Captains resigned their commissions, preferring to join Guérin in the ranks than hold them on such degrading terms. These and other matters caused the recall of Major-General Napier in 1848. He was succeeded by Major-General Bell, one of whose first acts was to reinstate, with their former rank, Captain Guérin, and the seven other officers who had resigned their commissions. This was the second condemnation of Guérin's dismissal, and then, for the first time, appeared the order, which had been kept secret by Napier: "That no officer should be dismissed in future without the express sanction of the Secretary of State."—*Tupper's "History of Guernsey," and others.*

---

10. *Mary Ann Collings*, m. 1st the Rev. George Birch (eldest son of George Birch, Esq., M.D., R.N.), Curate of St. Martin's, Birmingham, who died 1864 ; and 2nd, George Haynes Betts, Bey in the Egyptian Government service.

---

13. *Maria Matilda.*

Mary (dau. of Elias Guérin and Mary Arnold), m. John Bonamy ; issue, *John, Peter & Mary.*

1. *John*, m. Isabella Vardon : issue,
   1, *Isabella ;* and 2, *Henry*, who died unmarried.
   3. *John* (Lieut.-Col. Madras army), m. Jessie McCulloch ; issue, *Ella* and *Jessie.*
   4. *Maria*, m. a Mr. Hall.
   5. *Isabella.*
   6. *Louisa*, m. Edward Gardner; issue, *Ellen, Edward*, d., *Fanny, Allan.*
   7. *Martha*, m. Louis Chalen : issue, three children.

26

2. *Peter*, m. at Rio Janeiro, Miss Verguiro; issue, *John Verguiro, Isabella, Louisa Bonamy.*

---

3. *Mary*, m. John Collings (eldest son of John Collings, by Margaret Mauger, and brother of Mary Ann Collings, wife of Elias Guérin, of Le Mont Durant), and had issue,

  1. *Eliza Margaret*, d.

  2. *Bonamy*, Major R. G. M., m. Elizabeth D'Auvergne; issue, 1, *John Bonamy*; 2, *Charles D'Auvergne*; 3, *Gertrude Durell.*

  3. *Alfred*, Jurat, Royal Court, m. Matilda Lukis Collings; issue, 1, *Mary*; 2, *Henry*; 3, *Amy.*

  4. *Peter*, Rev., M.A., m. Jane Bird issue, 1, *Algernon William*; 2, *Ada Grace*; 3, *Godfrey Disney*; 4, *Cecil Bargrave*; 5, *Helen Maude*; 6, *Ernest Bonamy.*

4. *Susannah*, 5. *Nancy*, 6. *Eliza*, d. unmarried.

The family of Collings is descended from John Collings, of Ansford, in the Hundred of Collings, Co. Somerset, who came over to the Channel Islands in the year 1675, during the reign of Charles II. The present representative is Bonamy Collings, Major R.G.M., grandson of John Collings, by Margaret, his wife, daughter of Philip Mauger; and of Mary Guérin, wife of John Bonamy.—*Burke's "Illuminated Illustrations*, 1856."

The *Maugers* are descended from Mauger, Archbishop of Rouen, who was the son of Duke Richard II. of Normandy, by a noble Danish lady, and brother of Duke Robert, the father of William the Conqueror. William was but eight years of age on his father's death, and being illegitimate, Mauger was the lawful

heir to the Duchy, and was one of the most powerful opponents to the claims of his nephew; but the bar sinister in that age was not an insuperable obstacle to the succession to a throne. And although the Archbishop opposed William, they managed to get on very fairly together, and he was frequently consulted by the young Duke, to whom he is credited with having given sound advice and counsel. But in 1055, William much offended Mauger, by his marriage with Matilda, and the Archbishop excommunicated him, on the pretext that his wife was too nearly related to her husband. William was more exasperated by this than by all the pretensions of Mauger to the Duchy; and in the same year the Primate was deposed, and banished for life to the island of Guernsey, where according to Norman historians, he married or cohabited with a young lady of the name of Guille, by whom he had several children, and founded the family of Mauger of Guernsey. He is said to have resided at a place called "Saint," near Saints Bay, in the parish of Saint Martin in that island. He was drowned at sea, the body being found, and buried at Cherbourg."—*Tupper's "History of Guernsey," Lower, and others.*

His descendant, James Mauger, of Somerhuse (now Sommielleuse), in the parish of Forest, during the wars of England and France, started from the island of Guernsey, in the year 1419, with his men, landed at the little port of Agon, in Normandy, and captured by escalade the Castle of Mont Martin, near Coutances, on the 24th June. Henry V. of England was so pleased with this daring exploit, that he granted to James Mauger the Lordship of Bosque in Normandy (said by tradition to have been originally part of the possessions of the Archbishop Mauger his ancestor), and conferred upon him the distinguishing honour of adding to his paternal arms the Cross of St. George, in requital for his gallant and successful attack.

The patent is thus worded:—" In recognition of this feat of arms, the said James Mauger, Knight of Saint George, shall quarter on his arms, 1 and 4, d'argent a deux chevrons de sable, for Coutances, and 2 and 3 d'un lion rampant de sable, for Bosques;" and as a knight of Saint George, he bore the red cross of that order on his shield.

The Collings family quarter these arms with their own in conse-

quence of their descent from this James Mauger.—*Burke's " Illuminated Illustrations*, 1856."

The Maugers are said to have taken a very prominent part in the early history of the Channel Islands; and from the Archbishop the families of Mauger, Magor, Major, Mayor and Mayer claim descent.

From one of these sprang Sir Matthias Mayer, or Major, a Jerseyman, a soldier under Henry VII., who obtained a grant of arms, and lineal ancestor of R. Major, Esq., of Hurasley, Co. Hants, whose daughter, Dorothy, married Richard, afterwards Lord Protector Cromwell.—*Lower's " Patronymica Britannica."*

Margaret (daughter of Elias Guérin and Mary Arnold), d. unmarried.

Esther, their other daughter, m. Peter Solbé; issue :—

    1. Rev. *Guérin*, M.A., m. Miss De Lisle; he died in Smyrna, without issue.

    2. *Elias*, m. Miss de Jersey; no issue.

The remaining children, *Elisha, George, Mourant*, and *Sophia*, died unmarried.

MARY (the eighth child of Daniel Guérin and Marie Bacon), b. 1701, d. an infant.

JAMES (the ninth and last child of Daniel Guérin and Marie Bacon) was b. 1st March, 1706, and m. Mary Allez (of a Jersey family), by whom he had nine children, seven of whom died in infancy. His daughter

    1. *Mary*, m., 1st, Dr. Henry Forster, of Alnwick, without issue. By her second marriage with the

29

Rev. Simon James du Rozel, a Huguenot, native of Orleans, chaplain to the Queen, she had one son, *Frederick du Rozel*, a Commander R.N., who perished in the West Indies, on board one of H.M. ships; and a daughter, *Charlotte*, d. unmarried.

2. *Martha*, m. Jacob Marks, of Leamington. Issue, *Margaret*, *Esther*, *James*, and *John*, who all d. unmarried.

THE GUÉRINS OF DEVONSHIRE

Are a branch of the Guernsey Huguenot family.

Thomas Guérin, (third son of Elias Guérin and Mary Ann Collings, of Le Mont Durant, Guernsey,) was a Captain in the R.G.M., he died 1840; having married, April, 1829, Betsy, eldest daughter and co-heiress of Richard Read, of the Manor of Upton Helions, and Buxton, near Crediton; and of Brixington and Shortlands, near Exmouth, in the county of Devon; issue:—

1. *Marion Isabel*, d. 1862.
2. *Fanny Selina*, d. 1854.
3. *Emily*, m. Adam Wallace Elmslie, H.M. Acting Consul at Canton. Issue:—
   William Wallace.

4. *Thomas Read*, m. Ann Elizabeth, daughter of — Beaumont, of Nottingham, and widow of Major-General Huthwaite.

30

5. *Sidney Elizabeth.*

6. *William Collings Lukis*, m. Anna Maria, daughter of E. Edmonds, of Berrifield, Bradford, Wiltshire.

7. *Henry Adolphus*, d. 1855.

8. *Frederick Charles.*

The Devonshire family of Read have held property in the neighbourhood of Exmouth for many generations. Thomas Reed (as the name was then spelt) was Rector of Littleham cum Exmouth in the year 1666. On one of the bells he presented to the church 1692 the name is inscribed "Reade," but on his tombstone in the chancel, "Here lieth the body of Thomas Read, Rector of this parish 40 years, who died the 28th of March, 1706, aged 66."—*Webb's " Memorials of Exmouth."*

THE GUERINS OF SOMERSET

Are of the Champagne, Isle de France and Auvergne, family, which is divided into eight branches:

1st. Seigneurs de Champvoissi.

2nd. Seigneurs de Tarnaut.

3rd. Seigneurs de Brusland.

4th. Seigneurs de l'Huy.

5th and 6th. Seigneurs de Violaine.

7th. Seigneurs de Sauville.

8th. Seigneurs de Poisieux.

And these again into many minor branches.

They all bear similar Arms to the Mortagne, Clairac, Guernsey, and Devonshire Guérins, with the exception that *the lions are crowned.*

Since their settlement in England, the Somersetshire

family use the crest "a demi-lion crowned issuing out of a crown." They claim descent from *Robert Guérin*, (who, according to Hozier's Armorial, came originally from Brittany,) Seigneur de Poisieux, and father of Didier Guérin, Seigneur de Sauville. He married Damoiselle Jeanne Miron, by whom he had a son *François Guérin*, Chevalier, who was Lieutenant of Monseigneur le Marechal de Montmorency, Governor of Brittany, and Captain of the town and castle of St. Malo, 1521.

François married Damoiselle Anne de Fontenelle, by whom he had issue,

> *Leonard Guérin*, Chevalier, Seigneur de Poisieux de la Roche de Gastioni, de Chappes, et de Martreu, he married Marie de Crevant, by whom he had issue:
>
>> *Ambroise Guérin*, who married first Françoise d'Arcambourg, and had a son *Tanneguy*, who died without male issue. By his second marriage with Eleonore de la Trémouille, he had a son *Antoine*, and two daughters *Marie* and *Gabrielle*.
>>
>> *Antoine Guérin*, chevalier, Seigneur de Poisieux, de St. Croix, et des Essarts le Viscomte en Champagne, married Damoiselle Marguerite de Crevcœur, and by her had two sons, *Jacques* and *Louis*, and a daughter *Eleonore*.
>
> *Jaques Guérin*, chevalier, Seigneur de Poisieux, &c., was a Captain in the Light Cavalry Regiment of his Royal Highness. He married Damoiselle Marie du Creux, but had no children.

JOSEPH GUÉRIN supposed to be the descendant of *Louis*, and founder of the Somerset family, is said to have

arrived in England between the years 1750 and 1760, when, as a Protestant, he escaped from the Court of Louis Quinze. He married Jemima Saintsbury, and by her had three sons, and one daughter who died young, besides—

Joseph Guérin, M.A., of Trinity College, Oxford, Rector for many years of West Bagborough, and Norton Fitz-Warren, near Taunton, who by his marriage (1801) with Maria Lucy Eliza, eldest daughter of Arthur Lemuel Shuldham, of Dunmanway, County Cork, had one son and five daughters. He died in the year 1863, at the great age of 96.

1. *Catherine Maria*, m. the Rev. Richard T. Lowe, Chaplain of Madeira, now Rector of Lea, Gainsborough.

2. *Edmund Arthur*, Colonel E. I. C. S., who married in India, Louisa, daughter of Joseph Gilbert, issue:—

 1. *Joseph Arthur*, E. I. C. S., mar. Elizabeth Walker, daughter of the Rev. J. D. Oland Crosse, Vicar of Pawlett, near Bridgewater; issue, *Emily Maude*.

 2. *Emily Louisa*, m. Capt. Charles Frederic Keays. E. I. C. S., son of the Archdeacon of Bombay, by whom she had issue:—(1) *Frederic Edmund*, (2) *Evelyn Louisa Frances*, (3) *Henry Guérin*, (4) *Emily Maude*, (5) *Arthur Maitland*. She died at Kurrachee, in the year 1865.

33

3. *Emily Antonia*, m. the Rev. Thomas Orgill
Leman, Rector of Brampton, Suffolk.
4. *Lucy Frances*.
5. *Jemima Caroline*.
6. *Elizabeth Sophia*.

GUÉRINS OF CLAIRAC AND MAIRAC.

The information we have respecting Daniel Guérin's
family at Clairac is as follows:—The estate came into
the possession of Mrs. Guérin, his stepmother, and her
children, both through the continued absence of Daniel,
and also through an edict, whereby all the lands of the
Huguenots who had fled were confiscated.

The Guérins had for many generations continued on
the property, which they cultivated for the manufacture
of wines, and in the course of time amassed great
wealth. When Nicholas Guérin became the inheritor
of the estate, he being a man solely given up to
pleasure, squandered in dissipation nearly the whole of
his fortune, and died leaving several children, who,
although well educated, were in comparatively reduced
circumstances. With the money saved from the wreck
of their father's property, his two sons Nicholas and
Peter, with their younger brothers and sisters, emi-
grated to the West Indies, and purchased in the island
of St. Domingo an estate called " Plaisance," near Cape
Francis. The sisters all married. After many years'
residence in this colony, the two brothers, having
amassed a fortune, returned to France, being then the
sole survivors. Nicholas, with his daughter Theresa,

then about four years of age, settled at Clairac, and
Peter, who was unmarried, at Bordeaux. The latter
died, leaving all his property to Nicholas, who then
finally left Clairac and took up his permanent residence
at Bordeaux. His daughter Therese espoused Mons.
M. A. Plassan, a rich merchant of that town, by whom
she had one daughter, Clari, who is now the wife of
Mons. Amedié Meingot of Blaye. They having no
family, that branch of the Guérins of Clairac on her
death will become extinct.

Of the Guérins of Mairac but two were surviving in
the year 1843. Both possessed estates ; one was married,
but without issue. The other, his cousin, who had
been an officer under the Republic and the First Empire,
was unmarried. They had resumed the original name
as inscribed on the ancient title-deeds of the property,
which had been in possession of the family for nearly
four hundred years, and were then known as Messrs.
"Garin." On their deaths that branch also of the
Guérins of Guienne becomes extinct.

BACONS OF FAILAISE, NORMANDY.

The first intelligence received by the Guérins of Guernsey of Marie Bacon's family was between the year
1825 and 1828, when two Jersey gentlemen visited the
island on their return from Falaise, in Normandy,
where they had made the acquaintance of a Mons. Bacon
and his family ; M. Bacon, on hearing that they came

from the Channel Islands, inquired whether they knew
if there still existed in Guernsey a Huguenot family of
the name of Guérin, as his great-great-aunt had escaped
to that island on the Revocation of the Edict of Nantes,
and married a Mr. Daniel Guérin, also an émigré.

This Mons. Bacon and his family were in 1853 still
living on their estate, a few leagues distant from Falaise.

About the year 1841 or 1842 Mr. John Simon (whose
grandmother was Sarah Guérin, wife of Mr. Daniel Piton,
of Guernsey) was stationed at Battle Harbour, coast of
Labrador, in charge of a fishing station belonging to
merchants at Poole, when a Mr. Bacon, who was travelling in Canada, visited Battle Harbour, for the purpose of fishing and shooting, and became the guest of
Mr. J. Simon. Mr. Bacon having stated that he was
from Falaise in Normandy, he was informed by Mr.
Simon that very probably they were distantly related,
as his grandmother, Sarah Guérin, was descended from
Mr. Daniel Guérin of Clairac, in Agenois, who being a
Huguenot, fled to Guernsey, and there married, in 1686,
a Madlle. Marie Bacon, of Falaise, of a noble Norman family. Mr. Bacon gave an impression of his
Arms to be presented to the Guérins of Guernsey; which
is in the possession of Mr. Elias Thomas Guérin, of Le
Mont Durant.

The Bacons are one of the most ancient of the Norman
families, and there still exists a seigneurie of that name
in the province. William Bacon, 1082, endowed the
Abbey of the Holy Trinity at Caen.

The Bacons of Suffolk claim descent from one Grim-
bald, who came over to England with William the Conqueror, and settled near Holt, his great-grandson took
the name of Bacon, which his descendants have continued ever since.

36

Arms of the Huguenot and other Descendants of Guérins in England, &c.

The origin of the "lion" as a device used by the Guérins, is supposed to have been derived from Guérin, the first Count of Montglave, or Lyons, in the reign of Charlemagne. In the British Museum is a history of this "Guérin de Montglave," written by Michael Le Noir, tutor to the young Prince, and printed by the order of King Francis, in the year 1515, and it contains an old wood-engraving representing Guérin, as a knight in full armour, with sword and spear, guarding, with another knight, the tent of Charlemagne, over which are the Imperial Arms, "a Double Eagle displayed;" on Guérin's shield is "a Single *Crowned* Lion." By the kind permission of the Authorities of the Museum, I have been able to obtain a facsimile of this woodcut for a frontispiece.

This Guérin is said to have won the kingdom of France from the Emperor, about the year 808, at a game of chess (of which I will give full particulars hereafter), and many of the name, *his descendants* or *otherwise*, have, it may be, perhaps, in commemoration of the event, borne on their shields, some a lion or 3 lions; others 3 chess rooks or castles, as *Guérin de Rochemore;* and others, wholly or in part, a chequered board,* some adding to it the *one* lion, others the *three*—as for instance—the following English families who claim descent from Guérins of France—

---

* "This pattern was probably derived from the game of chess."
—*Glossary of Heraldry;* and also *Chess in Heraldry* in *Tomlin's Manual of Chess.*

1. Guérin, Count de Mont-
glave, or Lyons (*as in wood
engraving*).

2. Count de Lyons.

3. Guérin, " Election de
Mortaigne," Clairac. Guernsey, and Devonshire, &c.

Garein, Guarein	Chequey, Or et azure.
Garen and Garenne	,, ,,
Gearing and Gering	,, ,,
Warrens, Lion Rampant and ,,	,,
Warrens, 3 Lions Rampant, ,,	,,

Warington and Warrington, 3 Lions Rampant, counter-charged.

Warrington, 3 black Lions, Rampant on a gold shield (as a quartering).

Waring, Warring, 3 Lions passant, counter-charged.

The Earl de Warren, who came over with William the Conqueror bore Arms "Chequey, Or et azure," but his shield as represented at Castle Acre Priory, Norfolk, is "Checky," *black and white.*

Count de Garenne, who appears on the roll of Henry III., had the same "chequey, Or et azure."

John Warren, Bishop of Bangor, "Lion Rampant, a chief checky."

Warren, is the literal translation of the *Franco-Norman* name Guarin, which signifies "Keeper of a Warren." *French,* Garenne.

The present Count de Lyons, who claims descent from the first Count of Montglave, bears Arms—D'or d'un Lion de Sable, armés et langné de gueules.—(2.)

Guérin —"Election de Mortagne," Normandy. Arms, D'or à trois Lions de Sable, 2 and 1.— (3.)

The Town of Mortagne—Arms, "D'or à six Lions de Sable, 3, 2, and 1;" and the Arms of the family of Mortaine, in Leicestershire, are—"D'or à trois Lions de Sable, 2 and 1."—(3.)

38

1066.—*Miles de Guérin*—said to have accompanied William the Conqueror, and from him claim to be descended the Warings of Lancashire, the Warings of Waringstown, County Down, Ireland, and the Warringtons of Lancashire; these latter quarter with their Arms —" D'or à trois Lions de Sable, 2 and 1."—(3.)

Guérin, of Clairac, in Agenois, in Guienne, and their descendants the Guérins of Guernsey and Devonshire. Arms—" D'or, à trois Lions de Sable, 2 and 1."—(3.)

By the laws of Heraldry, " All Lions Rampant are armed and tongued red, unless *expressly* stated to the contrary." Therefore, these Lions should be described as " Armés et langués de gueules," as they are in the arms of the Count de Lyons, and the Guérins of Champagne, Isle de France, Auvergne, &c.

Guérin de Champagne, Isle de France and Auvergne; Seigneurs de Champoisi, de Tarnaut, de Brusland, de L'Huy, de Veilaine, de Sauville, de Trouville, de Poissieux, &c., &c.; also

Guérin, Seigneur de Beaumont, in Orleans; and the Guérins of Somersetshire (who use as a crest a Demi-crowned Lion issuing out of a crown) bear Arms—" D'or à trois Lions de Sable, 2 and 1. Armés, langués, et couronnés de gueules."—(4.)

No mention is made of the *three* Lions being crowned prior to 1500, and it is supposed they were assumed for the first time by Robert Guérin on his settling in Champagne and becoming Seigneur de Poissieux, and by his son, Didier Guérin, on his purchasing, 1541, the Seigneurie of Sauville, from Mons. Pierre Flamignon, and

4. Guérin de Champagne,
Isle de France, Auvergne,
Orleans, and Somersetshire.

5. Guérin D'Agon, Nor-
mandy.

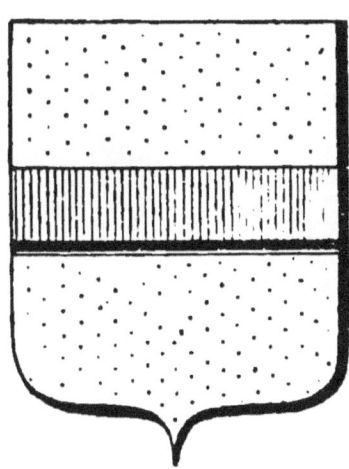

6. Guérin, Bishop of Senlis,
Chancellor of France.

7. Guérin de Flaux, Artois.

since that date the addition has been borne by their numerous descendants.

GUÉRIN, Bishop of Senlis, and Chancellor of France, a Knight of St. John of Jerusalem, bore no device on his Shield of Gold, but after the battle of Bovines, as a distinguished mark of honour, King Philip Augustus granted him the addition of a Band of Red across his shield, and in the " Salle des Croisades," Versailles, his Arms appear as " D'or à la fasce de gueules."—(6.)

GUÉRIN—Seigneur de Flaux, in Artois. Arms— " D'or, à trois chevrons d'azur accompagné en point d'un Lion de gueule au chef d'argent, chargé du trois étoiles d'or."—(7.)

GUÉRIN of Agon, in Normandy. Arms—" D'azur à trois Mollettes, d'éperon d'or, 2 and 1—Au chef d'or chargé d'un Lion naissant de gueules."—(5.)

These, as far as I can ascertain, are all of the name who bear Arms on *gold shields* or have the device of *one or more Lions*, and I think there is but little doubt that they sprang from one stock—the Guérins of Mortagne, in Normandy, who originally came from Auvergne.

Further details concerning the Arms and localities of other numerous branches of the Guérins I will try and make complete in the annexed biographical sketches.

BIOGRAPHICAL SKETCHES,

CHRONOLOGICALLY ARRANGED.

———

As it may not be without interest to those connected with these Huguenot families, I will add such information as I have been enabled to obtain respecting any bearing the name of Guérin, or Guarin, although in writing these sketches, I shall, in most cases, give merely an epitome of such particulars, together with, now and then, a cursory glance at the history of the period before us ; these I shall arrange chronologically.

The Guérins and Guarins, both French and Italian, have, as a race, in the course of ages given to the State many distinguished citizens, statesmen, soldiers, poets, painters, and men of letters and art. In the church the name has been particularly eminent; on its roll figure a Martyr, Saints, Cardinals, Archbishops, Bishops, Abbots, and numerous other dignities. Amongst the Crusaders they took a very prominent position, two being raised to the dignity of Prince as Grand-Masters of the Knights of St. John of Jerusalem, or Hospitalars, besides others as distinguished Knights of the Order.

The French "Guérin," and the Italian "Guérini," are the modernized nomenclature for the ancient " Warinus," "Warin;" "Guarinus," "Guarin;" "Gerin," and "Garin," which, as baptismal names, were in frequent use in the early ages, and are supposed to have been used in honour of a martyr whose name is thus variously spelt in the Chronicles of the Monasteries (but where these are copied at length by historians, as in the case of Mons. Martin Bouquet's "Histoire de France et de Gaul," an explanatory note states that " Guérin " is meant)*: this martyr suffered death by stoning in the year A.D. 500; and on the 5th October, 678, his name was placed on the list of the Roman Martyrology ; from which date he is always known as " Saint Guarin," or "Guérin," and from the great number so named, he would seem to have been held in special favour amongst ecclesiastics in the early ages.

" Warinus," and " Guarinus," are simply the French and Italian rendering of the Latin surname " Varinus,"† a name in frequent use amongst the Romans. In the early writings of Cicero mention is made of " P. Varinus, a Roman governor in Asia,"‡ and it is not improbable that this "Saint and Martyr " may have been a Roman citizen or soldier, domiciled in Gaul about the time of the Frankish invasion ; or perhaps one of the Varini, a very ancient people of Germany,† who may have come over with the Franks.

In the " Memoirs of G. Maurice de Guérin," by Mons. de Trebutien, it is stated that, " the founder of the family

---

* Bouquet's Hist., vol. 2, p. 450.

† Encyclopédie de Gens du Monde, p. 568 ; and Collier's Historical Dictionary.

‡ Lempriere's Classical Dictionary.

of Guérin, was one Guarini, an Italian, who settled in France early in the ninth century." After a careful examination into the matter I cannot coincide with this view, for I find in the Chronicles of the Monasteries in France mention of numerous Warins and Guarins as Abbots and Bishops, commencing as early as A.D. 674, also Counts of the name, and therefore I incline to the belief that they were the descendants of the Gallo-Romans; which seems borne out by Perry in his " History of the Franks," who remarks :—" What speaks more strongly than anything else for the belief in a gradual approach to equality in the positions of the Franks and the Gallo-Romans is, the indisputable fact that the office of Governor of a Gau or Canton was frequently held by a Roman. In Auvergne and Tours, the majority of the Counts were provincials."—Early as the reign of Pepin we have Counts Guarin and Warin, and a little later " *Warin, Count of Auvergne*," which, I think, is almost conclusive that Guarins were in France, holding a high position, long prior to the date given by Mons. de Trebutien, as to their migration from Italy.

In continuing this subject, in order to prevent confusion, I shall, with one or two exceptions, use only the modernized name Guérin, which has been in general use since 1500.

A.D. **674.** During the reign of Theodoric, or Thierri, son of Clotaire III.,—Ebrion being at the time Mayor of the Palace,—we have Leo de Garii, of whom mention is made in connection with his brother Guérin, an Abbot[*]— - (By a singular coincidence, this Guérin is said to have

---

* Bouquet's History, vol. 2, p. 630.

died on the very same day, 5th October, 678, on which
" Guarin" or "Gerin," his patron saint, was placed on the
Roman Martyrology).*

691. A GUÉRIN appears in a charter in conjunction
with Pepin, the Mayor of the Palace.†

745. GUÉRIN, Abbé of Antecombe, afterwards
Bishop of Sidon for forty years, of whom frequent mention is made during the reign of King Pepin,‡ was a man
renowned for his learning and piety. He is also spoken
most highly of, in a letter by Saint Bernard, one of the
great fathers and doctors of the church, the first Abbé
of Clairvaux, who was born 1091, and died 1153.§

760. Two Counts GUÉRIN are named in the lists of
the nobles and bishops who accompanied King Pepin,
when, together with his wife Bertrada, and his two sons, he
proceeded to a town on the Rhine, where a solemn service
was held in honour of the nativity of our Lord.‖

768. "The noble and illustrious Counts Cancor and
Guérin" are mentioned about the time Aquitaine was
re-annexed to the dominions of France ; this was almost
the last act of King Pepin, who died the same year.¶

771. COUNT GUÉRIN (supposed to be the same
man) appears on the list of nobles, &c., who attended on

* Bonquet's History vol. 2, p. 450.
† Vol. 3, p. 706.   Vol. 4, p. 676.
‡ Vol. 2, p. 697.   § Ree's Cyclopædia.
  Bonquet's History, vol. 5, p. 762.   ¶ Vol. 5, p. 352.

45

Carloman, when on a visit to Italy, of a similar purport to the one which he had made with his father, to celebrate with all pomp the nativity of our Lord. The king was taken ill during the ceremony, and died; he was succeeded by his brother Charles, afterwards Charlemagne. *

773 to 814. A GUÉRIN bore a very prominent part during the whole reign of Charlemagne. Some writers suppose that there were two, as it is hardly probable that it could be the same man who was alive at the death of King Pepin in 768. The principal deeds of this renowned warrior are to be found in a book entitled "L'Histoire de Guérin de Montglave," written by M. Michel le Noir, tutor to the young prince, by the order of King Francis, and printed in the year 1515. History and romance are so mixed up that it is difficult to draw a line as to what is fact and what fiction, but from it, it would seem that Guérin was engaged in nearly all the wars of Charlemagne. and especially in those against the Turks and Spaniards.

There is also an anecdote told † as to how Guérin became possessed of the title of "Count de Montglave," or Lyons. The story runs, that Guérin was a great player of chess (about that time (808) being first introduced into Europe), and the Emperor, who was equally fond of the game, considered himself without equal in his court, and challenged Guérin, saying :—

"I bet you would not play your expectations against me at chess, unless I were to propose some very heavy stake."

---

* Vol. 5, p. 715 and p. 18.

† L'Histoire de Guerin de Montglave; and in Charles Tomlin's Chess Manual.

46

" Done," replied Guérin. " I'll play, provided you stake against mine, your kingdom of France."

" Very good," said the Emperor, " let us see."

And the game commenced, its progress being watched with great interest by the assembled nobles.* Heavy bets are said to have been made as to the issue by the partisans on both sides. In the end, Guérin was declared the victor, and claimed the kingdom of France, but Charlemagne laughed the matter off as a joke. Guérin and his nobles were not at all disposed to look upon it in this light, and he swore, by all the saints of Aquitaine, that he must receive compensation. At last it was agreed that Charlemagne should surrender all his rights in the countship of Montglave, on consideration that Guérin should be able to take it from the Saracens, who then held possession. This he soon accomplished with the assistance of his powerful knights, capturing the place and taking prisoner Gasier, the Sultan, and his only daughter Mabiletta; her charms captivated his heart, and at her intercession, he saved her father's life on condition that both embraced Christianity; to this they agreed, and Guérin soon afterwards married Mabiletta, by whom he had four sons,† the eldest of whom is said to have become the Duke of Aquitaine.

---

* It is not improbable that this game may have been played with a set of ivory chessmen, which had been presented, about that time, to Charlemagne by the Empress Irene, of Constantinople, and are still preserved in the Cabinet of Antiquities in the Bibliothèque de Roy, at Paris.

† The adventures and victories of these four sons, who for wisdom and bravery against their country's foes by land and sea are unequalled, principally compose " L'Histoire de Guérin de Montglave;" but they are, of course, too lengthy to give in this sketch. Any one sufficiently interested in them will find a reprint

47

800. It was about this time that Charlemagne divided the kingdom into provinces, each territory to be governed by a peer, who was invested with a portion of the kingly power. To nine of these provinces the king appointed nobles whose forefathers had governed them, and amongst these we find Guérin, Count of Auvergne and Duke of Aquitaine,* whilst to the government of the remaining provinces the emperor appointed nobles of his own creation. These constituted the great peers of France—the first aristocracy—who after the death of Charlemagne were in reality the peers of the reigning king (not subjects), owners of provinces and dukedoms at times far exceeding in size the possessions of the nominal king, the yoke of whose authority was at once thrown off, or accepted, almost at the option of these powerful and formidable retainers.†

814 to **819.** On the death of Charlemagne and succession of his son Louis as emperor, the whole country was devastated by foreign wars and internal dissensions. And in the latter year, Guérin, Count of Auvergne, and Berengier, Count of Toulouse, gave battle to Lupus Centules, a count of the illustrious house of Gascony, when at the head of a large army he rebelled against Louis; after a very protracted fight Lupus was defeated and taken prisoner, his brother Gesame being killed.‡

---

of the story in either " Collections des Romans de Chevaliers," by Alfred Delvau, Paris, 1869, or the " Bibliothèque B. Universelle des Dames," at the British Museum.

* E. Baluze's Histoire Généalogique de la Maison d'Auvergne.

† General histories.

‡ Bouquet's, vol. 6, p. 141, and Sismondi's History, &c., &c.

48

A.D. **830** to '35. GUÉRIN, Count of Auvergne, we find in open rebellion against the Emperor on Louis' refusal to comply with his demands. He was joined by Count Lambert and other nobles, and they seized the Empress Judith, during her stay at Notre Dame à Loon, as a hostage, and tried to compel Louis to grant their requests, in which they failed; nevertheless, this rash act in no way seems to have interfered with the friendship of the Emperor for Guérin; and when, a few years later—833— the three ungrateful sons of Louis dethroned their aged father and divided the Empire amongst them, the Count of Auvergne and his cousin, the Count of Burgundy, placed themselves at the head of the discontented nobles, and defeating the three sons, replaced Louis on his throne, where they upheld him to the day of his death.* Guérin was rewarded for his part in Louis' restoration by a confirmation of the grant of the dukedom of Aquitaine; and when Judith's son, Charles, was made king of that province, 835,† we find Guérin styled "Duke of Aquitaine, also Duke of Toulouse, under whom was Egfridus, Count of Toulouse."

841. On the death of the Emperor Louis, his three sons disputed the division of the Empire, which they endeavoured to decide in the following year, 842, by force of arms, in the bloody battle on the plains of Fontenoy,‡ memorable for the great number of the slain, of whom upwards of one hundred thousand men were left on the field.§ The Duke of Aquitaine took a very prominent

---

* Sismondi's History. Bouquet's History, vol. 7, p. 31.
† Vol. 7, p. 31, Notes A and B.   ‡ Vol. 7, p. 223.
§ Bouquet's History, vol. 7, p. 598.

part in this struggle, and all the chronicles speak most
highly of the wisdom and valour he displayed, and adjudge
to him the honour of the victory. The result of this
engagement was that Italy was assigned to Lothaire ; Germany to Louis ; and France, with Burgundy, to Charles ;
while Guérin was confirmed in the possession of the
Dukedoms of Aquitaine and Toulouse, thus becoming one
of the most potent and influential of the great peers.*

849. GUÉRIN, a rich and powerful Abbot † in
Alsace, of warlike reputation, who flourished during the
reigns of the Emperor and his sons.

The chronicles for the next hundred years contain little
but a confused medley of battles, and negotiations patched
up between the Great Dukes and Counts, wars and spolia-
tions never ceasing throughout France—might was the
only right acknowledged. It was about this time that
the founders of the families of Guérin in Normandy and
Brittany are supposed to have made their way north, and
settled in those provinces.

984.‡ GUÉRIN was Archbishop of Cologne at the
time of the coronation of Hugh Capet (3rd July, 987),
and a GUÉRIN,§ Abbot of St. Michael, also is noticed
as occupying a prominent position in the stirring events
of that period.

1029.§ GUÉRIN was Bishop of Beauvais during the
stormy occurrences which marked the reign of Henry I.,

---

* Bouquet's History, vol. 7, pp. 225, 377.   † Vol. 9, p. 276.
‡ Vol. 9, p. 250.   § Vol. 10, and other histories.

and especially in that monarch's war with Eudes, Count of Champagne and the Count of Flanders ; and again, when Stephen, Count of Champagne, and Thibaud, Count of Touraine and Beauvais, revolted in 1037. The Bishop is said to have used all his influence to bring about a reconciliation, but without effect, and the confederates were defeated. Thibaud purchased his freedom by renouncing Touraine, and Stephen his, by the loss of the greater part of his lands.

1030 to '35. GUÉRIN (eldest son of William Talvas de Bellesme, Count of Alençon, Sens, &c.), together with his brothers Fulk, Robert, and William, ravaged the Duchy of Normandy in revenge for the capture of their father's capital by Robert I., sixth Duke of Normandy (father of William the Conqueror), in consequence of the Count of Alençon's refusal to do him homage and fealty, and to take the usual oath of fidelity. Fulk was killed, and Robert wounded, in this conflict. Robert became afterwards Earl of Alençon, but was taken prisoner, and died in confinement.*

What became of Guérin is not stated, but it is not improbable that on his father's death he became possessed of Sens, one of his father's numerous countships, and that a branch of his descendants may have used his christian as a surname—although the family name was Talvas—for from that date we have *Guérins*, Viscounts, Counts, and Barons de Sens, down to the time of Anne Giles de Guérin, Baron de Sens, and Marquis de St. Brice, 1671.

1066. TURSTIN DE GUÉRIN (or Guéron, as it is sometimes written,) appears on some of the lists of the

---

* Morery and others.

celebrated Battle Abbey Roll, of those taking part in the Battle of Hastings. *

MILES DE GUERIN is said to have accompanied William the Conqueror in his expedition ;† and from him claim to be descended the Warings of Lancashire, the Warings of Waringstown, Co. Down, Ireland, and the Warringtons of Lancashire,‡ these latter quarter with their arms the " three black lions on a gold shield," of the Guérins, "Election de Mortague," Normandy.

1070. GUÉRIN, the son of Gaston, a gentleman of Dauphiny. About the end of the eleventh century they, father and son, founded a hospital for the reception of sick pilgrims who came to visit the body of St. Antoine, which Josselin had brought from Viennois. It was this which gave rise to the Order of St. Antoine, which was approved of by Urban II., in the Council of Clermont, in the year 1095. For two hundred years this order was governed by seventeen superiors, who took the title of " Master." Aimoin de Montagne was the first who received the title of " Abbé," from Boniface VII., in the year 1297. §

1096. GUÉRIN DE ROCHEMORE, one of the knights who, under the banners of the Count of Toulouse, so distinguished himself in the first crusade, 1096. He took a very prominent part in the siege of Archas, of which mention is made in the chronicles of Robert le Moine ; and he is also named in the charter of Hugh,

---

* " Le Nobiliaire de Normandie," by Le Vicomte de Magny— and " Chronicques de Normandie" by Léopold de Lisle.

† Burke, and others.   ‡ Burke's Illustrations, 1844.

§ Morery.

52

Count of Jaffa,* on the lists of the contemporaries of
Gerard, founder of the Order of the Knights of Saint
John of Jerusalem, or Hospitalars. His Arms, " D'azur,
à trois rocs d'echiquier," are placed with those of three
other Guérins in the " Salle de Croisades " at Versailles.†

1103. GUÉRIN, Archbishop of Arles,‡ during the
reign of Philip, and his son Louis, of whom there is
little of importance to relate.

1180. GUÉRIN, Archbishop of Bourges, and GUÉRIN,
Viscount of Sens, were amongst those present at the
coronation of Philip Augustus, by the Archbishop of
Sens.§

1187. GUÉRIN DE MONTAIGU,¶ as a Hospitalar,
took part in the fatal battle of Tiberias, in which the Crusaders were totally defeated by Saladin, and the true cross
captured by the Saracens. Soon followed the fall of Jerusalem, which after a defence of fourteen days was captured
and the banners of the victor planted on the walls of the
city. But the career of Saladin was afterwards checked by
the resistance of Tyre, where were assembled, 1189, all the
Christian troops which had capitulated at Jerusalem,
amongst them the Knights Hospitalars under Jeffry le
Rat, and Guérin de Montaigu, whose forces were daily

---

* Major Porter's Knights of Malta.
† Galeries Historique, &c., Versailles.
‡ Bouquet's History, vol. 12. § Bouquet's History.
¶ Various histories — Mills, Porter, De le Boisgelin, &c.;
Morery's Hist. Généalogique de Familles Illustres.; Bosio, Hist. de
l'Ordre de St. Jean de Jerusalem ; Naberat, Priviléges de l'Ordre.

augmented by the arrival of succours from Genoa, Pisa, France and Normandy. From Tyre the Christians proceeded to Acre, to which they lay siege for upwards of one year; Saladin and his hosts were encamped but a few miles' distance, and harassed the besiegers in every possible way, till the Christians, although victorious in many a bloody encounter, began to sink under despair, as their ranks were gradually thinned by the sword, famine and disease. But in the following Spring, 1190, their spirits were revived by the arrival of Philip of France, and Richard of England, whose appearance caused dismay to the Saracens. All the attempts of Saladin to raise the siege were repelled by the vigilance of the Christians, and Acre was soon after captured. It was for the great bravery and wisdom displayed by Guérin, that on the death of Jeffry le Rat he was chosen Grand Master of the order. At this siege France lost the Counts of Flanders, Bar, Blois, Sancerre, Eu, and Ponthieu, besides a long list of nobles of inferior rank, but equal courage. During the dispute as to the empty title of "King of Jerusalem," Philip with the Templars supported the pretensions of Conrad, Marquis of Montferrat, and Richard, with the Hospitalars, that of Guy of Lusignan. This unseemly quarrel was eventually settled by the latter, retaining for life the crown of Jerusalem.

Of this Guérin de Montaigu, as Grand Master of the Knights of St. John, more hereafter.

1190 to 1230. GUÉRIN*; Bishop of Senlis, Chancellor of France, and Frère Guérin, are the titles by

---

* C. Desbois, Major Porter, Mills, Crowe, Morery's Dictionary Généalogie de Familles Illustres; Bigord's Life of Philip Augustus; P. Anteul's Hist. des Ministres; and others.

which this distinguished man is most generally known. He is spoken of by all historians as one of the wisest men of his age. In his early youth he was a Knight Hospitalar. It is uncertain whether he was engaged in the battle of Tiberias, and fall of Jerusalem ; but if so, he had returned to France prior to Philip's quitting it, to rescue the Christians, for he was amongst those left in charge of the kingdom as a councillor of state during the absence of the king ; on whose return Guérin became his chief companion and adviser. In 1203 he was appointed Abbot of St. Victor, in Paris, and in the same year, Keeper of the Seals. He is said to have been a man of great ambition, and that he induced Philip to attempt the conquest of Normandy; which was effected the following year, 1204. At his instigation, also, the arms of France were engaged in extending the dominions and augmenting the authority of Philip, who was nothing loth to take the double advantage of gratifying the ambition of Pope Innocent III., whilst adding to his own power, in attacking the possessions of Raymond, Count of Toulouse, a man of noble mind, and even in those early days an advocate for unbounded religious toleration amongst his subjects. The result is well known in the Crusade against the Albigenses, to which flocked the chivalry of Europe, as it brought them greater gains and less trouble than the Holy Wars. It ended in the spoliation of Raymond, a large portion of whose land fell to the share of Philip.

In 1213 Guérin was consecrated Bishop of Senlis, and this honour was conferred on him as a reward for the wisdom of his counsels to the king in the management of the state, whereby the most important changes had been

brought about and the hitherto separate interests of the feudal nobles were converted into a confederation of powers strictly subordinate to the Crown. A tumultuous republic of barons and knights became a well-balanced kingdom, with local privileges and a centralised authority, whilst the communes were rich and flourishing.

1214. As a general, Guérin is chiefly renowned for the strategy he displayed in the management of the troops at the battle of Bovine, 24th July, although he took no actual part in the conflict. In this battle Philip is supposed to have had about fifty thousand men, led by the Duke of Burgundy, the Counts of Dreux, Nevers, Sancerre, Ponthier, and St. Paul; whilst the German army, under Otho, their emperor, is estimated at from two to three hundred thousand, under the commands of the Dukes of Limburgh, Brabant, and Lorraine, and the Counts of Namur, Flanders and Bologne, together with the English Earl of Salisbury. The conflict was fierce and bloody, and the issue for a long time doubtful, the fortunes of France and Germany alternately prevailing. Philip was wounded in the throat by an arrow, and falling from his saddle, was nearly dragged to death by his horse. It was after this event that Guérin had the sole disposition of the troops, and he placed the French with their backs to the sun, whilst it dazzled the eyes of their adversaries, and one by one every post was carried; at last the German army beat a hasty retreat, ending in a tumultuous flight. All historians greatly extol the wisdom and courage displayed by Guérin on this occasion.

For the next few years he devoted the whole of his abilities to various reformations throughout the kingdom; and on the death of Philip Augustus, 1223, he was nominated executor to the will of the king. On the

accession of Louis VIII. to the throne, Guérin was appointed "Chancellor of France," the dignity of which office he is said to have revived in all its former splendour, making its holder take rank as one of the great peers of the realm, and first of all the officers of the Crown.

On the death of Louis, 1226, he was joint guardian with Queen Blanche of the young king, then only eight years of age. And when some few years later many of the great nobles and vassals, dissatisfied with their gradual loss of power, and the growing strength of the lower classes under the privileges they now enjoyed, endeavoured to seize the queen regent and the young king, the chancellor, with the now powerful and armed people, headed by a few of the faithful nobles, hastened to their rescue, and defeated the confederate barons.

In the year 1228, Guérin resigned all his dignities into the hands of the queen and the young king Louis IX., and retiring to the Abbey of Chalis, became a monk of the order; he died at the age of 70, two years later, and was buried on the left hand side of the grand altar of the monastery: where his tomb may still be seen.

He bore no device on his shield of gold, but after the battle of Bovine, as a distinguishing mark of honour, Philip Augustus granted him the addition of a band of red across the shield; and his Arms now appear in the "Salle de Croisades" at Versailles, as "D'or à la fasce de gueules."

A.D. **1208** to **1230**. GUÉRIN DE MONTAIGU,*

---

* Major Porter, De le Boisgelin; Ancient and Modern Malta; Morery, Dict. Généalogique de Familles Illustres; Bosio, Hist. de l'Ordre de St. Jean de Jerusalem, &c.

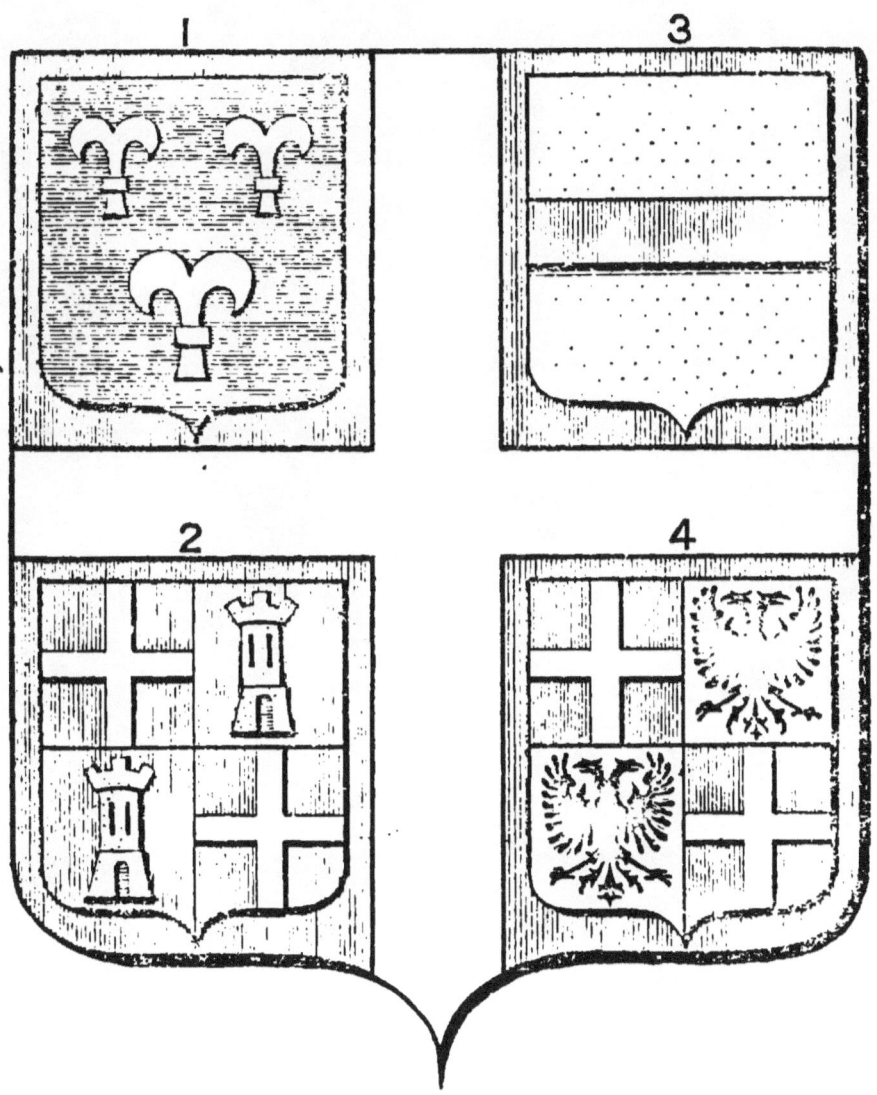

THE ARMS OF GUÉRINS, KNIGHTS HOSPITALAR, IN THE "HALL OF THE CRUSADERS," AT VERSAILLES.

1. GUÉRIN DE ROCHEMORE.

2. GUÉRIN DE MONTAIGU—14th *Grand Master.*

3. GUÉRIN—Bishop of Senlis, Chancellor of France.

4. GUÉRIN of Provence—16th *Grand Master.*

These arms have not been adopted by any of the families of the name.

who for the distinguished part he had taken in the wars against Saladin, was chosen 14th Grand Master of the Knights of St. John of Jerusalem, on the death of Jeffry le Rat.

He had hardly been appointed to this important post before hostilities were commenced between Simon, King of Armenia, and the Count of Tripoli, concerning the principality of Antioch ; at the request of Pope Innocent III., the Grand Master at the head of his Hospitalars allied himself with the king, whilst the Templars— between whom and the Hospitalars a feeling of bitter enmity existed—went over to the side of the Count of Tripoli ; and for two years this war raged between them with varying success. The Turks, profiting by the internal quarrels of the Christians, entered Armenia with a powerful army, and laid siege to various fortresses. The Hospitalars were thus attacked on both sides ; but Guérin concentrating his forces, threw himself and his devoted knights suddenly and unexpectedly on the Turks, following up his successes so quickly, that he raised the siege of each fortress, and gained such a decisive victory that it ended in the total defeat of the foes, and all their camp and treasure fell into his hands, as they fled from the country. He then renewed, with redoubled vigour, the war against the Count of Tripoli, which obliged him to conclude a temporary peace. The King of Armenia, desirous of giving proof of his appreciation of the gallant defence of his country, handed over to Guérin, on behalf of the order of the Knights of St. John, the towns of Salef, Chateauneuf, and Carnodo ; which gift was afterwards confirmed by the Pope, 1211.

In 1217, Guérin accompanied Andrew, King of Hungary, to Cyprus. The king had brought over large rein

forcements to the help of the Christians in Palestine ; he expressed a great wish to be admitted as a knight of the Order, bestowing on the Hospitalars 500 marks of silver from the resources of his kingdom, and a further 100 marks, towards the expenses of the Chateau de Crae, then in possession of the knights.

In the following year occurred the crusade against Egypt ; and it was at the sieges of Damietta in May, 1218, and November, 1219, that Guérin and his knights brought such renown on the order of the Hospitalars as to rank them with the foremost amongst men so celebrated for their heroism as the Counts of Nevers and La Marche, the Archbishop of Bordeaux, the Bishops of Meaux, Autun, and Paris, under whom the French crusaders fought—and those of England, fighting under the command of the Earls of Chester and Arundel ; William Longespée, Earl of Salisbury (son of King Henry II. by fair Rosamond) ; the Baron Harcourt, and other great warriors. From Egypt, Guérin returned to Cyprus, and for the next few years devoted all his energies to setting in order the affairs of that kingdom, which had been greatly neglected.

In 1222, he visited Rome in company with the King of Jerusalem, who went to arrange with the Pope a marriage between his daughter Violante and the Emperor Frederick. The Pope was so pleased with the important reforms effected by Guérin in the government of Cyprus, that he placed the island under the sole charge and care of the man who had shown himself so capable of ruling, making him virtually king thereof ; this was confirmed by a brief dated 1226, and he continued to hold the government of the island until his death, 1230. After the excommunication of the Emperor Frederick II.

he refused, equally with the Templars, to pay allegiance, or obey the orders of that prince. Guérin was Grand Master of the Hospitalars for three and twenty years, and a knight of the order for upwards of fifty; thus enjoying his dignities for a longer period than any other knight since the death of the venerable Raymond du Puy. He died full of honours, having merited and won the respect of all the Christian princes. His Arms, " Ecartelé aux 1 et 4 de la religion, et aux 2 et 3 de gueules à la tour d'or," are emblazoned in the " Salle de Croisades " at Versailles.*

A.D. 1231 to '36 or '44.† GUÉRIN of Provence was nephew of the last Grand Master; he had been engaged under his uncle as a Knight Hospitalar in the crusade against Egypt and the siege of Damietta. He

---

* Galeries Historiques, Versailles.

NOTE.—There have been some doubts expressed as to whether the correct appellation for this prince is Guérin, or De Montaigu, but a careful examination into the matter soon clears up the apparent uncertainty. *Montaigu* is a small town, crowned by a castle, situated in the mountains of Auvergne, and was one of the many possessions of the Guérins of that province. *Guérin de Montaigu* was so called to distinguish him from Guérin, Bishop of Senlis, and Guérin, of Provence, afterwards the 16th Grand Master, who were all Knights Hospitalar, about the same time.

Major Porter, in his work on the " Knights of Malta or Hospitalars," introduces him as Guérin de Montaigu, but afterwards only makes mention of him as "Guérin." De le Boisgeline, in " Ancient and Modern Malta," says, " Guérin was born in Auvergne." And his portrait as one of the Guérin family was in the possession of the father of G. Maurice de Guérin du Cayla, who claims him as ancestor.

† Louis Morery; Bosio, Hist. de l'Ordre de St. Jean de Jerusalem; Naberat, Priviléges de l'Ordre, and others.

succeeded Bertrand de Texis as 16th Grand Master in
the year 1231 or '32 ; and according to a charter of the
26th October, it was to this prince, and not to his succes-
sors, that Pope Gregory recommended the interest of the
Emperor Frederick II. He used all his influence in en-
deavouring to allay the feeling of enmity and jealousy
subsisting between the Templars and the Hospitalars, in
which cause he sacrificed both his liberty and life.

The town of Ascalon in Palestine was under the protection of the Templars. It was besieged by the Corasmins, or Kharismians (a people who came out of Scythia,
having been driven from Persia). This vast horde
traversed Arabia, plundering and laying waste all the
towns on their route ; and when at length they attacked
Ascalon, the Templars sent to beg assistance from the
Hospitalars ; and Guérin, without having regard to the
late bitter feeling and hatred existing between the two
orders of knights, but considering only the good of the
Christian cause, placed himself at the head of the Hospitalars, and being joined by Gauthier, Count of Jaffa
(brother of the King of Jerusalem), and his followers,
gave battle to the Corasmins, who, after a desperate conflict,
were defeated and put to flight, leaving in the hands of
the Christians their camp, and its vast treasures, the
pillage of Arabia. The attention of the knights was now
turned to secure this plunder, and whilst laden with
the spoils, which they were removing to the town of
Ascalon, the Corasmins, on their swift horses, returned, and
renewed the battle ; the knights having no time to form,
and being in a state of utter disorganization, fell an easy
prey to their enemies, who, thirsting for revenge and the
re-capture of their treasures, fought with desperation ; the
Christians were utterly routed, the greater number of

them being slain or taken prisoners; amongst the latter were the Grand Master Guérin and the Count of Jaffa, who were sent to Soudan in Egypt, and from that moment all is lost in obscurity concerning Guérin. It is even unknown whether he was still in bondage or whether he had been ransomed at the time of his death; as to the date of which historians differ, but ranging from 1236 to 1244. His Arms, "Ecartelé aux 1 et 4 de la religion, et aux 2 et 3, D'argent à l'aigle eployée de sable," are also at Versailles. He was a nephew of Guérin, the Chancellor of France, and brother of Guérin Guérin, Seigneur of Ponzols, in Auvergne, and of

1257. WILLIAM DE GUÉRIN,* Count de Brionde and chorister in the church, from which he took the title. In the thirteenth century the dignities of this celebrated church of Brionde in Auvergne were exclusively possessed by the children, or the brothers, of the Counts and the Dauphins of Auvergne, the Counts of Clermont and the Viscounts Polignace, and could only be held on proof being given that for four generations on both father's and mother's sides their descent was noble. And Mons. Cheney Desbois, in his "Dictionnaire de la Noblesse," argues that if William de Guérin had not been able to prove direct descent from the Counts of Auvergne he could not have been a chorister, which was the fifth dignity of the church, and had been held thirty years before by William de la Tour, whom the French kings recognised as the descendant in direct male line from the ancient Dukes of Aquitaine and Counts of Auvergne.

---

* C. Desbois.

62

1240. GUÉRIN D'APCHIER a troubadour who flourished at the Court of Adelaide of Toulouse, niece of Louis the Young; he married Blanche, daughter of the Dauphin of Auvergne.*

1340. GUÉRIN DE GUY, bishop, was a very celebrated monk of the order of St. Dominic, in Languedoc, a man of great learning; he was Doctor of Theology, in Paris, in 1333, and author of many works, amongst others, an abridged life of Saint Marguerite, daughter of the King of Hungary.†

1364. JEAN GUÉRIN, of whom mention is made as *one of seven* out of the two hundred knights who fought with Bertrand du Guesclin, Constable of France, during the wars which made his name so famous in history. These seven are singled out for their very conspicuous gallantry, and as being the bravest of brave men, who for daring and courage were unequalled in the field. Guérin is supposed to have been taken prisoner, together with du Guesclin and other of his knights, by the Black Prince at the battle of Navarette, 1367.‡

1396. EON GUERIN appears on the list of knights who fought under Viscount de Rohan, during the wars of this period.§

1420. JEAN GUÉRIN was one of the principal ministers of the Dauphin Charles, Regent of France.‖ He

---

* Trebutien's Maurice de Guérin.
† Louis Morery.
‡ Desbois and other writers. § Ibid. ‖ Ibid.

was especially chosen to recover the person of the young
Duke of Brittany, who had been seized by the Countess
Penthièvre. Her father, the Constable Clison, had been
left guardian to the little duke, and during a temporary
absence of the constable the child was seized by the
Countess, with the intention of placing her own son in
power in his stead. Guérin obtaining possession of the
young duke, her plans were thwarted. We next find
him (1427) named as one of the one hundred and nine-
teen nobles, who defended Mont Saint Michel against
the English under the Duke of Bedford.

1420. JEAN DE GUÉRIN,* another noble whose
name appears in connection with the history of Lorraine,
principally as Controller of the Purse of Reignier or René,
Duke of Lorraine and King of Sicily ; he died about the
year 1460, and was succeeded by his son Jean de Guérin,
who held the same post.

1437. ALAIN DE GUÉRIN appears on the list of
nobles taking the oath of fidelity to the Bishop of St.
Malo ; and in similar acts of the nobles of Montcontour
and Guëldo, we have Jean Guérin and Eon Guérin
respectively.*

1427 to **1513.** We find several Guérins, who are mentioned in their quality of nobles, as being exempt from
fouages, or hearth-money.*

1450 to **'53.** After the final loss of Normandy to the
English, Charles VII. made an expedition against the
nobles who still adhered to the cause of England, in

---

* C. Desbois, &c.

64

Guienne; and amongst the nobles of Normandy who joined his standard and took part in the siege of Bordeaux and Bayonne, are supposed to have been some of the Guérins de Mortagne; as the arms of the Guérins of Clairac, the ancestors of Daniel Guérin, the Huguenot who escaped to Guernsey, are the same as those of the Guérins de Mortagne, (as already described.) and the title-deeds held by the Guérins of Mairac had, in 1843, been in the possession of the family for upwards of four hundred years, just coinciding with this conquest. On the capture of the above-mentioned towns, Guienne, after an interval of three centuries, was reunited to the crown of France.

1540. WILLIAM GUÉRIN, Advocate-general of the Parliament of Aix in Provence, was one of the commissioners deputed by the Jesuits to execute the edict against the Vaudois Huguenots. He perpetrated the greatest cruelties against these unfortunate victims during the carnage he ordered in the surrounding villages; but a just judgment soon overtook him, he was brought before the Parliament of Paris by the seigneurs of the villages he had pillaged, and was condemned, not, it is said, for his cruelties, but for falsehood, calumny, and prevarication, and beheaded in the year 1554. It is said that on the same day and hour of this execution his wife, who was still at Aix, saw the figure of the head of her husband imprinted on her hand.*

1563. JACOB GUÉRIN, with his wife and children

---

* Dezobry and Bachelet, Manual Biography, History; Louis Morery Dict. Généalogique de Familles Illustres; and others.

from Normandy, were the first Huguenots of the name who fled to England. They were one of eighteen families who came over with their pastor, Hector Hamon, and landed at Rye, in Sussex, and were the founders of the " French Huguenot Church " still existing in the crypt of Canterbury Cathedral.*

1567. CLAUDE DE GUÉRIN, minister and secretary of state during the reign of Duke Charles III. of Lorraine, and President of the Chamber of Nobles 1595.†

1600. YVES DE GUÉRIN, Gentleman of the Chamber to Henry IV. King of France ; on the tragic death of that monarch, he retired entirely from public life, residing on his estates.†

1606. GILLES GUÉRIN, a sculptor of great renown ; amongst his most esteemed works was a bas-relief in the King's Chamber at the Louvre, representing " Fidelity, Authority, and Justice," and Apollo and two beautiful horses at the fountains at Versailles. He died in the year 1678.‡

1618. ANTOINE DE GUÉRIN took a very prominent part in the siege of Candie, during an assault on which he was killed by a cannon-shot.§

1671. ANNE GILES DE GUÉRIN, Baron de Sens, and Marquis de St. Brice. Minister of State, during a great part of the reign of Louis XIV. ‖

---

* Smiles' Huguenots, and others.   † C. Desbois.
      ‡ Bouillet's Dictionnaire Universel.
   § C. Desbois and others.   ‖ C. Desbois.

66

1666. CLAUD DE GUÉRIN, Baron de Lugeac. Endowed a vicarage to the church of Brionde, with 5,000 francs (£200) a year for ever, to be held by a priest of the name and arms of Guérin—failing whom, to a gentleman proving noble descent, on both father's and mother's sides, for at least four generations.*

1678. PETER GUÉRIN.† A learned French Benedictine Monk, born at Rouen in Normandy. At the early age of eighteen he took the monastic vows, and made such proficiency in the Greek and Hebrew languages, that he was appointed professor of them in the seminary belonging to his order. He was the author of a Hebrew grammar and a Hebrew lexicon. He died at Paris, 1729, in the monastery of St. Germain-des-Pres, of which he was the librarian, aged fifty-one years.

1682. SIMION GUÉRIN, and DANIEL GARIN or GUÉRIN,‡ were naturalized in England by letters patent.

1685. DANIEL GUERIN, of Clairac, in Agenois, in Guienne, fled from his home during the persecutions of the Huguenots at the revocation of the Edict of Nantes. He settled in Guernsey, and was the founder of the families of the name, in that island, from whom also are the Guérins of Devonshire.

1688. FRANCIS GUÉRIN, § his wife and children, and *Nicholas Guérin*, Huguenots, naturalized by letters patent.

---

* C. Desbois.   † Rees' Cyclopædia, Wilkes' Cyclopædia.
‡ Camden Papers.   § Ibid.

67

1691. GILBERT AGATHANGE DE GUÉRIN,* Baron de Lugeac, et de Bueil, was page to King Louis XIV.

1697. SOLOMON DE GUÉRIN, and Anne his wife, Huguenots, naturalized by letters patent.

1702–45. PIERRE DE GUÉRIN, Abbé of Vezelay. In 1724 was consecrated Archbishop, and Prince of Embrun; in 1739, Cardinal, and Abbé de Trois Fontaines, and of St. Paul of Verdun ; 1740, Archbishop and Count of Lyons, and Prelate Commander of the Order of St. Esprit. In 1742 he became Minister of State. He died 1757 ; his brother Claude, two years later, being the last of the Guérins of Dauphiny and Savoy.†

1750 to '60. JOSEPH GUÉRIN, of Champagne and Isle de France, founder of the Somersetshire family of the name, fled from the Court of Louis Quinze, and settled in England.

1758. CHRISTOPHE GUÉRIN, a celebrated engraver ; his principal works were " Venus desarmant l'Amour," after Corregio ; " L'Ange conduisant Tobié," after Raphael; "La Danse des Muses," after Jules Romain. He died in the year 1830.

1760. JOHN GUÉRIN, brother of the former, was a miniature painter of great distinction. He died 1836.

1764. PIERRE NARCISSE GUÉRIN, a pupil of J. B. Regnault, was a very noted historical painter.‡ Amongst his works the most famous are those painted in 1796—

---

* C. Desbois.   † C. Desbois and others.
‡ Morery, Bouillet, Dezobry and Bachelet, and numerous others.

68

" Le Corps de Brutus rapporté à Rome," "Caton d'Utique déchirant ses Entrailles," " Le Retour de Bélisaire dans sa Famille ; " in 1800—" Marcus Sextus ; " 1802— " Phèdre et Hippolyte ;" 1810—" Bonaparte pardonnant aux Revoltés du Caire," and " Andromaque ;" 1817— " Enée et Didon," " Egisthé," and " Clytemnestre ;" and in 1822—" La Mort de Priam " and " Sainte Genevieve," which latter has been copied in Gobelin tapestry, and is also used as one of the banners of the Church. , In this same year he was appointed director of the French Academy at Rome ; and on his retirement in 1829 he was made member of the Order of St. Michael, officer of the Legion of Honour, and created a baron of France. He died at Rome in the year 1833. All his works have been engraved ; " Cephæstus and Aurora," and " Æneas recounting the fate of Troy," by Forster.

1783. JEAN BAPTISTE PAULIN GUÉRIN,* more generally known as Paulin Guérin, was born in the south of France. He was a very distinguished painter, his works being principally of a religious character, although many are mythological. His " Cain after the death of Abel," 1812, was purchased by the French Government, and hangs in the Palace of the Luxembourg. His " Descent from the Cross," obtained a gold medal 1817, and was purchased by King Louis XVIII., and by him presented to the Roman Catholic Cathedral in Baltimore, U.S. The Government also purchased his " Anchises and Venus." " Ulyssée en butte au courroux de Neptune," 1824, is in the Museum at Rennes. " Adam and Eve driven from

* Bouillet's Dict. Univ. Hist.; Partington's; and Ripley's and Dana's Cyclopædias, and many others.

the Garden of Paradise," 1827, "Le Dévouement du Chevalier Roze," 1834, are hung at Marseilles. And in 1844 he painted "The Conversion of Saint Augustine." His chief portraits were those of Charles X. and Lamennais. He died in the year 1855.

1790. GABRIEL CHRISTOPHE GUÉRIN, son of the engraver, Christophe Guérin, was also an historical painter; his chief work was "Le Mort de Polynice," 15 ft. by 12 ft., for which he obtained the gold medal at the Louvre, 1817; it was afterwards hung at the Strasburg Museum.

His brother, Jean Guérin, was also a painter of distinction.

1810. GEORGES MAURICE DE GUÉRIN, a young French poet,[*] was born of a poor but noble family in the south of France; he was educated in Paris, and at the close of 1832, went to join Lamennais in his retirement at La Chesnaye in Brittany; he remained there about a year, but although he seemed to recognise the noble character, and to believe in the mission of Lamennais, he left comparatively untouched by his teachings, and uninterested in his aims. For the next few years, the problem how to live was the trouble of his life; but his marriage to a rich lady in 1838 promised to set him free from such cares; his health, however, failed, and he died of consumption within a year. His journal, letters, and poems, were published in 1862, by Mons. de Trebutien, who also wrote his memoir, which excited much interest, not only in France, but in England and other countries. His

---

[*] Maunder's Biographical Treasury.

principal compositions are the prose poems entitled, "Le Centaure" and "La Bacchante," in which, with much grace and melody, he expresses what he supposes was the Greek feeling and thought respecting nature and the world. From childhood he shewed a singular and profound susceptibility to the beauties of nature and the world, and a fondness for dreamy speculation. He was of a religious temperament, but seems not to have had latterly any definite belief in Christianity.

EUGÉNIE DE GUÉRIN. His sister was five years older than himself. She was a woman of equally remarkable character. The love of her brother was the predominant element of her life ; it was such a pure. deep, and absorbing love as is most rarely seen. She was a fervent Catholic, and saw with pain the loosening of her brother's hold on his early belief. She kept a journal, which was intended for his perusal alone ; it has been published since her death, and read with great interest.

This family of Guérin were known as the De Guérins du Cayla, and are descended from Jean de Guérin, Seigneur de Rinhodes, who, in 1534, on his marriage with Jeanne de Lapeyre, daughter and heiress of the Seigneur du Cayla, assumed the arms of that family. The father of Maurice de Guérin had in his possession a portrait of Guérin de Montaigu, as Grand Master of the Hospitalars.

71

GUÉRIN OR GUÉRINI, OF ITALY.

It will not be without interest if I add particulars of the Italian family of Guarin or Guarini, Guérin or Guérini, especially as the French Guérins are said to be descended from them. They, like the French, commence with a "Saint."

12th Century. GUÉRINI Cardinal.*—Some say he was of the noble family of Foscari, and others of the Guérinis of Bologne. He embraced a religious life contrary to the wishes of his parents, and shortly afterwards entered as one of the regular canons of the order of Saint Augustine, where as a strict recluse he passed the life of a saint. He was made Cardinal, and Bishop of Palestine by Pope Lucius II., 1144 or 5. These dignities were accepted by him much against his wish, and they did not hinder him from persisting in the austerity of his former life, and he secretly sold the valuable gifts presented him by the Pope, and distributed the money amongst the poor. He built the hospital of " St. Job." During the troubles in Italy he returned to his bishopric, and died at the great age of 110 years. The order of Saint Augustine had the sanction of the Pope to commemorate the memory of Guérini as one of their saints.

1370 – 1460. GUÉRINI, "OF VERONA,"* as he is usually styled, was a man of renowned learning. At the

---

* Louis Morery and other writers.

early age of twenty he sailed for Constantinople, and became a pupil of Manual Chrysoloras, and on his return he settled in Verona, and became one of the most accomplished teachers of literature in Venice. He was the first man of his nation that ever taught publicly the Greek language in Italy, and he was the first to discover and favour mankind with the poems of Catullus. From Verona he afterwards went to Ferrara, and is by many called a Ferrarese. By order of Pope Nicholas V. he wrote the lives of Aristotle and of Plato; and he translated into Latin, amongst others, the works of Plutarch and Strabo, and also wrote an abridgement of the Greek grammar of Chrysoloras. He died 1460. *Jean Baptiste Guérini*, his son, succeeded him as professor of Greek at Ferrara, and of him Paul Tore says, " he was, if anything, more learned than his father."

1537 to **1612**. JEAN BAPTISTE GUÉRINI (or Guarini, as he is called by the Italians) was the grandson of Jean Baptiste Guérini of Ferrara, and born in 1537. He was secretary to Alphonse, Duke of Ferrara, who intrusted him with several important commissions, as ambassador to various courts. After the death of that prince he was successively Secretary of State to Vincent de Gonzaya, to Ferdinand de Medicis, Grand Duke of Tuscany; and to Francis Maria de Feltré, Duke of Urbino. He was looked upon as an excellent statesman, and of that eminence for his wit that most of the academies of Italy made him a member of their society. He was well ac-

* Partington's British Cyclopædia; Ripley and Dana's Cyclopædia; Morery; Collier's Historical Dictionary, and many others.

quainted with polite literature, and acquired lasting repu
tation by his poems, especially by his "Pastor Fido," the
most admired of his many works, and of which there have
been innumerable editions and translations into almost
all the European languages. He died 1612.

ALEXANDER GUÉRINI, son of John Baptiste, was
in the service of Alphonse II., Duke of Ferrara. He went
as ambassador to Tuscany, and afterwards to the Court of
the Duke of Modena, from which as envoy to Venice.
He afterwards went to Vienna and Bavaria as ambassador
on behalf of Ferdinand, Duke of Modena.*

1626. CAMIELLE G. GUÉRINI.— A celebrated
architect; his chief productions are, at Paris, the church of
"Sainte Anne;" at Lisbon, the church of " Sainte Marie de
la Providence;" at Venice, the church of " Saint Gaëtan;"
at Turin, the palaces of the Prince Royal and the Prince de
Carigan, the Chapel Royal, the church of "Saint Lau-
rent," the College of the Nobles, and the gate of the Po.†

1630 to '83. MOINE THÉATIN GUÉRINI.—A
man of great learning, flourished in the seventeenth century. He was mathematician to the Dukes of Savoy and
Modena. In 1666 he published in Paris his "Placita
Philosophica," and died in 1683.*

---

* Morery. † Bouillet's Dictionary of Universal History.

74

Summary of the French Families of Guérin, and their Arms.

I will conclude with a short summary of the various branches of the Guérins of France, their different localities, titles, and arms. Historians say, "that without doubt, the families of the dukes and counts, to whom with the king, belonged the sovereignty of France, have extended themselves through a series of centuries, connected with all the remembrances of French glory, from the remotest periods of its history, even, down to the present day." And this is true of the family of Guérin, who all claim descent from the ancient counts of Auvergne and dukes of Aquitaine, although in the course of generations, in various branches, they have by conquest, grants, and matrimonial alliances, spread themselves throughout the kingdom, forming distinct families and bearing different Arms.

773 to 814. GUÉRIN, Count of Auvergne, frequently styled "Duke," was granted the Countship of Montglave or Lyons in payment of a debt, he having, it is said, won the kingdom of France from the Emperor Charlemagne at a game of chess. His Arms, according to a woodcut in L'Histoire de Guérin de Montglave, appears to have been a "*lion armed, tongued, and crowned*," but no heraldic colour is given to the shield or the device. His eldest son was afterwards Duke of Aquitaine, and the arms of that dukedom "un lion passant gueules," were added to those of Henry II. on his marriage with Eleanor, Duchess of Aquitaine, and now form part of the royal arms of England.

75

The present Count of Lyons, who claims descent from this first Count of Montglave, bears arms, *D'or, d'un lion de sable, armes et langué.*

Having given a full description of the Arms of the families using the *gold shield*, and *the lion*, or *lions*, including those of Mortagne, Clairac, Champagne, Isle de France, Auvergne, Orleans, Agon, Artois, Guernsey, Devonshire and Somersetshire, I need not repeat it here, but will continue with the other branches.

AUVERGNE.

Guérin, Marquis de Lugeac, Baron de Lugeac, Count de Bueil, Seigneur de Ponzols, Chambarel Chazlan, Busscol, Lavaudier, Marsat, St. Genest, La Tourette, Roches, &c., &c. Arms, Losangé d'argent et de sable ; à la bordure de gueules.

From these Guérins are said to be descended the ancient earls of Salisbury and many branches of the Montagues in England.

In the roll of Henry III., 1245, we have the Arms of Warin (or Guérin) de Monchensy and William Montague, both " D'argent à trois lozenges de gueules."

And amongst the clergy who bore as Arms the *three lozenges,* either black or red, we have

Simon Montacute, Bishop of Winchester, 1337 to 1345
James Montague, Bishop of Bath and Wells, 1608 to 1616
George Monteigne, Bishop . . . . . 1617 to 1621
Richard Mountague, Bishop of Chichester, 1628 to 1638
Mountaigue, Bishop of Westminster, 1613
George Montaigne, Archbishop of York, who died 1628.

76

BRITTANY.

Guérin, Marquis de St. Brice, Baron de Sens and Seigneur de la Grasserie, de Belotiere, de l'arigne, Champinel, de la Fontaine, &c.—Arms, D'azur au chevron d'or, accompagné en chef de trois besant du même, à la bordure engrêlée d'argent.

Guérin de la Grée.—Arms, D'azur, au sant d'argent, cant, de quatre flammes d'or.

Guérin de Frontaigné, Maine.--Arms, De gueules à trois écussons d'or.

Guérin de la Landelle.—Arms, De gueules, au chef d'argent, chargé de trois mouches d'hermine de sable.

LORRAINE.

Guérin, Count de Blamont, Seigneur de Montel, Neuvre, and Hermamesnil. Arms, D'argent à la poir te d'or, chargé d'une croix potencée d'azur, et accompagnée en chef de deux autres croix potoncées d'or—Extinct since 1612.

LANGUEDOC.

Guérin, Seigneur de Tournel. — Arms, Tranché de gueules et d'argent.

NORMANDY.

Guérin.—Arms, D'azur à trois palmes d'or, au chef consu de gueules, chargé de trois roses d'argent.

PROVENCE.

Guérin, Seigneur de Fuveau. —Arms, De gueules à la colombe essorant d'argent, bequée, et membrée d'or.

Guérin, Seigneur de Cayla.—Arms, De gueules, à six besant d'argent, 3, 2, et 1, au chef consu d'argent. *Extinct.*

77

SAVOY AND DAUPHIN.

Guérin, Seigneur de Tencin.—D'or à l'arbre de sinople, au chef de gueules chargé de trois besants d'argent. And another branch of the same family bears Arms. D'or au Laurier arrache de Sinople, au chef de gueules, chargé d'une étoile d'or, coloyée de deux bessant du même. Both extinct since 1759.

Then we have the

Guérins, in Querey, Seigneurs d'Ois; in Rouergne Seigneurs de Rinhodes ; in Gévaudeur, Seigneurs d'Apechier, the Seigneur de Saignes; and others, of whom I have been unable to obtain the Arms.

Many of the Arms borne by the families of Guérin have been assumed on marriage with heiresses, or otherwise.

Though *not unknown* with French arms, the crest is of very uncommon occurrence ; in place of it the armorial shield is surmounted by a coronet, or casque, denoting the title or rank of the family ; with the exception of the Guérins of Somersetshire none of the families of the name use the crest, simply the Arms with the casque or coronet.

The " de " of the noblesse was in general use before the name Guérin until the Huguenot persecutions, but it was dropped by the émigré families, and also most generally by the French families during the revolution of 1793.

After the flight of the Huguenots, at the revocation of the Edict of Nantes, acts were framed by nearly all the provincial parliaments throughout France for securing the properties of those who had remained faithful, or

had been converted to the Catholic religion. They were
called " Acts for the Reformation of the Noblesse," and
in them, amongst others, the families of Guérin were
declared " Noble, and their issue of noble extraction, and
it is permitted to them and their descendants to take the
legal quality of esquire, and to bear arms."[*]

---

[*] C. Desbois and others.

WATERLOW AND SONS, PRINTERS, GREAT WINCHESTER STREET, E.C.